SEXTET

SEXTET

ACKNOWLEDGMENTS

Illustrations for "On Turning Eighty" by Bob Nash of Big Sur, California, drawing of Hydra harbor by Kathleen Mackintosh, cover photograph by Edgar W. D. Holcomb.

Library of Congress Cataloging in Publication Data

Miller, Henry.
  Sextet.

  CONTENTS: On turning eighty.—Reflections on the death of Mishima.—First impressions of Greece. (etc.)
  I. Title.
PS3525.I5454S4   813'.5'2   77-20795
ISBN 0-88496-119-2
ISBN 0-88496-111-7 pbk.

CAPRA   PRESS
631 State Street, Santa Barbara, CA 93101

SEXTET

ON TURNING EIGHTY
REFLECTIONS ON THE DEATH OF MISHIMA
FIRST IMPRESSIONS OF GREECE
WATERS REGLITTERIZED
REFLECTIONS ON THE MAURIZIUS CASE
MOTHER, CHINA AND THE WORLD BEYOND

HENRY MILLER

Capra Press / 1977 / Santa Barbara

4538

CONTENTS

EDITOR'S NOTE

No one more than Henry Miller has contributed to the founding and perpetuation of Capra Press. Our first book to demand any literary attention was Henry's "On Turning Eighty" which he wrote for us in a gesture of friendship dating back to our Big Sur days together in the 50s. I was an amateur stonemason then, hauling stones for his garden walls on Partington Ridge and reading all the books he generously passed on to me. I little suspected then, that the day would come, nearly 20 years later, when I would be one of his publishers.

It's been our good fortune, since 1972, to have published a series of Miller's shorter works. Each was a memorable event for our press and each was designed in the spirit of glad spontaneity. That explains why these six little books, though born of the same parent, vary so much in size and shape. Being such slender volumes, however, they were often overlooked or lost on bookstore shelves.

Here we bring them together under one cover, yet seeking to retain a sense of their original form. We hope you enjoy the diversity of Miller's writing as much as we do. Think of yourself as holding six lively personalities living peacefully together under the family name, SEXTET.

N.Y.

ON TURNING EIGHTY

Journey to an Antique Land

Foreword to

The Angel is My Watermark

by

HENRY MILLER

1972

On Turning Eighty

I F AT EIGHTY you're not a cripple or an invalid, if you have your health, if you still enjoy a good walk, a good meal (with all the trimmings), if you can sleep without first taking a pill, if birds and flowers, mountains and sea still inspire you, you are a most fortunate individual and you should get down on your knees morning and night and thank the good Lord for his savin' and keepin' power. If you are young in years but already weary in spirit, already on the way to becoming an automaton, it may do you good to say to your boss—under your breath, of course—"Fuck you, Jack! you don't own me." If you can whistle up your ass, if you can be turned on by a fetching bottom or a lovely pair of teats, if you can fall in love again and again, if you can forgive your parents for the crime of bringing you into the world, if you are content to get nowhere, just take each day as it comes, if you can forgive as well as forget, if you can keep from growing sour, surly, bitter and cynical, man you've got it half licked.

It's the little things that matter, not fame, success, wealth. At the top there's very little room, whereas at the bottom there's plenty like you, no crowding and nobody to egg you on. Don't think for a moment that the life of a genius is a happy one. Far from it. Be thankful that you **are** a nobody.

If you have had a successful career, as presumably I have had, the late years may not be the happiest time of your life. (Unless you've learned to swallow your own shit.) Success, from the worldly standpoint, is like the plague for a writer who still has something to say. Now, when he should be enjoying a little leisure, he finds himself more occupied than ever. Now he is the victim of his fans and well wishers, of all those who desire to exploit his name. Now it is a different kind of struggle that one has to wage. The problem now is how to keep free, how to do only what one wants to do.

Despite the knowledge of the world which comes from wide experience, despite the acquisition of a viable everyday philosophy, one can't help but realize that the fools have become even more foolish and the bores more boring. One by one death claims your friends or the great ones you revered. The older you grow the faster they die off. Finally you stand alone. You observe your children, or your children's children, making the same absurd mistakes, heart-rending mistakes often, which you made at their age. And there is nothing you can say or do to prevent it. It's by observing the young, indeed, that you eventually understand the sort of idiot you yourself were once upon a time—and perhaps still are.

One thing seems more and more evident to me now—people's basic character does not change over the years. With rare exceptions people do not develop or evolve: the oak remains an oak, the pig a pig, and the dunce a dunce. Far from improving them, success usually accentuates their faults or short-comings. The brilliant guys at school often turn out to be not so brilliant once they are out in the world. If you disliked or despised certain lads in your class you will dislike them even more when they become financiers, statesmen or five star generals. Life forces us to learn a few lessons, but not necessarily to grow. Off-hand I can think of only a dozen or so individuals who learned the lesson of life; the great majority would not recognize their names if I were to give them.

As for the world in general, it not only does not look any better to me than when I was a boy of eight, it looks a thousand times worse. A famous writer once summed it up thus: "The past seems horrible to me, the present gray and desolate, and the future utterly appalling." Fortunately, I do not share this bleak point of view. For one thing, I do not concern myself with the future. As for the past, whether good or bad, I have made the most of it. What future remains for me was made by my past. The future of the *world* is something for philosophers and visionaries to ponder on. All we every really have is the present, but very few of us ever live it. I am neither a pessimist nor an optimist. To me the world is neither this nor that, but all things at once, and to each according to his vision.

---

*Joris Karl Huysmans, author of *Against the Grain*.

At eighty I believe I am a far more cheerful person than I was at twenty or thirty. I most definitely would not want to be a teen-ager again. Youth may be glorious, but it is also painful to endure. Moreover, what is called youth is not youth, in my opinion; it is rather something like premature old age.

I was cursed or blessed with a prolonged adolescence; I arrived at some seeming maturity when I was past thirty. It was only in my forties that I really began to feel young. By then I was ready for it. (Picasso once said: *"One starts to get young at the age of sixty, and then it's too late."*) By this time I had lost many illusions, but fortunately not my enthusiasm, nor the joy of living, nor my unquenchable curiosity. Perhaps it was this curiosity—about anything and everything—that made me the writer I am. It has never left me. Even the worst bore can elicit my interest, if I am in the mood to listen.

With this attribute goes another which I prize above everything else, and that is the sense of wonder. No matter how restricted my world may become I cannot imagine it leaving me void of wonder. In a sense I suppose it might be called my religion. I do not ask how it came about, this creation in which we swim, but only to enjoy and appreciate it. Much as I may rail about the condition of life in which we find ourselves I have ceased to believe that I can remedy it. I may be able to alter my own situation somewhat but not that of others. Nor do I see that anyone past or present, however great, has been able to truly alter *"la condition humaine."*

What most people fear when they think of old age is the inability to make new friends. If one ever had the faculty of making friends one never loses it however old one grows. Next to love friendship, in my opinion, is the most valuable thing life has to offer. I have never had any trouble making friends; in fact, it has sometimes been a hindrance, this facility for making friends. There is an adage which says that one may judge a man by the company he keeps. I often wonder about the truth of this. All my life I have been friends with individuals belonging to vastly different worlds. I have had, and still have, friends who are nobodies, and I must confess they are among my best friends. I have been friends with criminals and with the despised rich. It is my friends who have kept me alive, who have given me the courage to continue, *and* who have also often bored me to tears. The one thing I have insisted on with all my friends, regardless of class or station in life, is to be able to speak truthfully. If I cannot be open and frank with a friend, or he with me, I drop him.

The ability to be friends with a woman, particularly the woman you love, is to me the greatest achievement. Love and friendship seldom go together. It is far easier to be friends with a man than with a woman, especially if the latter is attractive. In all my life I have known only a few couples who were friends as well as lovers.

Perhaps the most comforting thing about growing old gracefully is the increasing ability not to take things too seriously. One of the big differences between a genuine sage and a preacher is gayety. When the sage laughs it is a belly laugh; when the preacher laughs, which is all too seldom, it is on the wrong side of the face. The truly wise man—even the saint!—is not concerned with morals. He is above and beyond such considerations. He is a free spirit.

With advancing age my ideals, which I usually deny possessing, have definitely altered. My ideal is to be free of ideals, free of principles, free of isms and ideologies. I want to take to the ocean of life like a fish takes to the sea. As a young man I was greatly concerned about the state of the world; today, though I still rant and rave, I am content simply to deplore the state of affairs. It may sound smug to speak thus but in reality it means that I have become more humble, more aware of my limitations and those of my fellow man. I no longer try to convert people to my view of things, nor to heal them. Neither do I feel superior because they appear to be lacking in intelligence. One can fight evil but against stupidity one is helpless. I believe that the ideal condition for humanity would be to live in a state of peace, in brotherly love, but I must confess I know no way to bring such a condition about. I have accepted the fact, hard as it may be, that human beings are inclined to behave in a way that would make animals blush. The ironic, the tragic thing is that we often behave in ignoble fashion from what we consider the highest motives. The animal makes no excuse for killing his prey; the human animal, on the other hand, can invoke God's blessing when massacring his fellow men. He forgets that God is not *on* his side but *at* his side.

Though I am still quite a reader I have come more and more to eschew books. Whereas in the early days I looked to books for instruction and guidance, today I read primarily for enjoyment. I can no longer take books, or authors, as seriously as I once did. Especially not books by "thinkers". I find such reading deadly now. If I do tackle a so-called piece of serious writing it is more to seek corroboration than enlightenment. Art may be therapeutic, as Nietzsche said, but only indirectly. We all need stimulation and inspiration, but they can be had in many different ways, and often in ways which would shock the moralists. Whichever path one takes it is like walking the tightrope.

I have very few friends or acquaintances my own age or near it. Though I am usually ill at ease in the company of elderly people I have the greatest respect and admiration for two very old men who seem to remain eternally young and creative. I mean Pablo Casals and Pablo Picasso, both over ninety now. Such youthful nonagenarians put the young to shame. Those who are truly decrepit, living corpses, so to speak, are the middle-aged, middleclass men and women who are stuck in their comfortable grooves and imagine that the *status quo* will last forever or else are so frightened it won't that they have retreated into their mental bomb shelters to wait it out.

I have never belonged to any organization, religious, political, or otherwise. Nor have I ever voted in my life. I have been a philosophical anarchist since my teens. I am a voluntary exile who is at home everywhere except at home. As a boy I had a number of idols, and today at eighty I still have my idols. The ability to revere others, not necessarily to follow in their footsteps, seems most important to me. To have a master is even more important. The question is how and where to find one. Usually he is right in our midst, but we fail to recognize him. On the other hand I have discovered that one can learn more from a child very often than from an accredited teacher.

I think the teacher (with a capital T) ranks with the sage and the seer. It is our misfortune not to be able to breed such animals. What is called education is to me utter nonsense and detrimental to growth. Despite all the social and political upheavals we have been through the authorized educational methods throughout the civilized world remain, in my mind at least, archaic and stultifying. They help to perpetuate the ills which cripple us. William Blake said: *"The tigers of wrath are wiser than the horses of instruction."* I learned nothing of value at school. I don't believe I could pass a grammar school test on any subject even today. I learned more from idiots and nobodies than from professors of this and that. Life is the teacher, not the Board of Education. Droll as it may sound, I am inclined to agree with that miserable Nazi specimen who said: *"When I hear the word Kultur I reach for my revolver."*

I have never been interested in organized sports. I don't give a damn who breaks what records. The heroes of baseball, football, basketball are virtually unknown to me. I dislike competitive games. I think one should play not to win but to enjoy the game, whatever it be. I prefer to get my exercise through play rather than through doing calisthenics. I prefer solo performance to team work. To swim, to ride a bike, to take a walk in the woods, or to play a game of ping pong satisfies all my need of exercise. I don't believe in push ups, weight lifting or body building. I don't believe in creating muscles unless they are to be used for some vital purpose. I think the arts of self-defense should be taught from an early age and used for that purpose only. (And, if war is to be the order of the day for the next few generations, then we should stop sending our kids to Sunday School and teach them instead to become expert killers.)

I don't believe in health foods and diets either. I have probably been eating all the wrong things all my life—and have thrived on it. I eat to enjoy my food. Whatever I do I do first for enjoyment. I don't believe in regular check-ups. If there is something wrong with me I'd rather not know about it, because then I would only worry about it and aggravate the condition. Nature often remedies our ills better than the doctor can. I don't believe there is any prescription for long life. Besides, who wants to live to be a hundred? What's the point of it? A short life and a merry one is far better than a long life sustained by fear, caution and perpetual medical surveillance. With all the progress medicine has made over the years we still have a pantheon of incurable diseases. The germs and microbes seem to have the last word always. When all else fails the surgeon steps in, cuts us to pieces, and cleans us out of our last penny. And that's progress for you.

What is so woefully missing in our world of today are grandeur, beauty, love, compassion — and freedom. Gone the days of great individuals, great leaders, great thinkers. In their place we are breeding a spawn of monsters, assassins, terrorists: violence, cruelty, hypocrisy seem to be inbred. In summoning the names of illustrious figures of the past, names like Pericles, Socrates, Dante, Abelard, Leonardo da Vinci, Shakespeare, William Blake, or even the mad Ludwig of Bavaria, one forgets that even in the most glorious times there was unbelievable poverty, tyranny, crimes unmentionable, the horrors of war, malevolence and treachery. Always good and evil, ugliness and beauty, the noble and the ignoble, hope and despair. It seems impossible for these extreme opposites not to co-exist in what is called a civilized world.

If we cannot better the conditions under which we live we can at least offer an immediate and painless way out. There is the escape through euthanasia. Why is it not offered the hopeless, miserable millions for whom there is no possible chance of enjoying even a dog's life? We were not asked to be born; why should we be refused the privilege of making our exit when things become unbearable? Must we wait for the atom bomb to finish us off all together?

I don't like to end on a sour note. As my readers well know, my motto has always been: "Always merry and bright." Perhaps that is why I never tire of quoting Rabelais: "*For all your ills I give you laughter.*" As I look back on my life, which has been full of tragic moments, I see it mor᷍ as a comedy than a tragedy. One of those comedies in which while laughing your guts out you feel your heart breaking. What better comedy could there be? The man who takes himself seriously is doomed.

The tragedy which the vast majority of human beings is living is another matter. Therein I see no comic element of relief. When I speak of a painless way out for the suffering millions I am not speaking cynically or as one who sees no hope for mankind. There is nothing wrong with life itself. It is the ocean in which we swim and we either adapt to it or sink to the bottom. But it is in our power as human beings not to pollute the waters of life, not to destroy the spirit which animates us.

The most difficult thing for a creative individual is to refrain from the effort to make the world to his liking and to accept his fellow man for what he is, whether good, bad or indifferent. One does his best, but it is never good enough.

Finis

Journey to an Antique Land

TRAVELING ABOUT in the south of France last year I had occasion one day to visit St. Rèmy. In the space of a few hours I had two wonderful surprises; first, the discovery of the house in which Nostradamus was born; second, a glimpse of the remains of a Greco-Roman settlement, Glanum, at the edge of the town. Heading towards the ruins I came upon a signpost reading 'Les Antiques'. An arrow indicated the direction of the site. Arrived at the spot, I was suddenly reminded of the work of Bob Nash. True, the road leading to it was a little firmer, a little stouter, than the slender monorails which Nash employs; but the arrow and the vestiges of a city that once was were definitely Bob Nash.

One of the fascinations about ruins is that they always suggest or reveal the original layout, the intention, in other words. In the midst of utter dilapidation one is certain to come upon isolated pieces of perfection: an arch, a pillar, a cupola, a paving block. With the work of restoration not only are the charm and the mystery dissipated, but the effect, a simulacrum, is that of *rigor mortis*. Nothing ever looks as it once did. Time is the passionate master of decomposition. Creation and destruction are twins, as once were love and justice.

Why do I talk ruins and destruction? Because there is fascination in them. Because, if one is sensitive and nostalgic, they make poems. The gleaming Empire State Building, descendant of an endless line of perfected monsters, must await the poets of death. Like the Sphinx with its missing nose it must attend the mutilations of time before it can capture the eye of the poet.

Journeying to that antique land which is the theme of these thousand and one "ideolinear" dreams, one is impressed by the vast amount of material which Nash has jettisoned. His line, seismographically sensitive, often leaves in its wake an ectoplasmic residuum, as well as a few striated boulders shaped like marbles. It is a line which approaches the lapidary abstractions of the mathematician. A geophysical tremor pervades it — evidence of the mysterious and unpredictable *elan vital* which even rocks, in birthing, register. It is a line which, no matter how delicate or tenuous, can as well support a trilobite as an airy eggshell. One meets with it occasionally in a Picasso, in the curve of a shoulder or the swift fall of a haunch. One finds it again in a piece of frayed string which some child has left beside a discarded top. It is not a line, really, but an intention. It demonstrates the illimitable impulses of the heart, whether in connecnection with the human figure, the house of Atreus, or the shifting positions of the constellations.

My first contact with Nash's finding — one can't speak of them as miniatures because they defy dimensional description — left me with a feeling of mystification. What was the man trying to say? And why, for example, had he not reduced them to the size of postage stamps? After I had seen a hundred or so I realized that he was size was perfect, even when it deviated a few millimetres this way or that.

Living each day with a new batch, they finally invaded my dreams. I would be starting a journey, homeward usually, and there were these calling cards lying all about me in the hot, waste desert. A mere glance at one and my orientation was immediately established. They were like so many broken threads dropped by some absent-minded Ariadne. Often the insuperable obstacle in my path was nothing more than the feather of a mythical bird, a feather which leaned at a perilous angle and seemed impervious to the ruthless winds that alter the face of the desert. Sometimes I had to climb over a sunken temple, as would an ant over a huge, rotting turnip. Occasionally gigantic cliffs rose up before me like frozen mastiffs, and in the dream my heart would pound before I had even raised myself a foot. Endless were the detours, the culs-de-sac. And then — typical irrelevant question— what was so strange, after all, about those boulder-balls to the right and left of the line of march? Nothing. They existed in the primeval ooze as well as in the trackless paths of dying meteorites; they could be found in any molecule, in the fibre of the nerves, in a spider's web. Even more were they to be met with in the mind. As were the amnesic boats which sailed without water, which rose and fell away like sand dunes — or the froth issuing from the mouth of an epileptic. Also in the fleshy and javelins, the mnemonic ruins, as it were, of ancient massacres. And moons, always crescent-shaped, always deplaced, as if on leave from other heavens, other aeons of time. The line, tremulous and ever-sensitive to inner disturbances, rose and sank along fevered horizons stabbed by spars and rigging of sightless ships. In short, all was familiar and recognizable, though part of history had crumbled away. The terrain itself, fragmented, etiolated though it was, was what one remembered of it. Antique to the vanishing point, it was nevertheless exasperatingly accessible. It had affinities with other known lands, but only as maps and charts relate to voyage and geography. A pre-Mercator world, compounded of Cambrian fugues and Jurassic minuets.

The line of the poet, and Nash is definitely a linear poet, always bears the stigma of prefiguration. As one who has traveled all the roads and highways, Nash has dispensed with all encumbrances, even the abracadabra of ideation. Idea itself has been honed to a razor's edge. His pictographic messages, rendered in ideolinear code, seem to come from the hidden face of the moon. He has thoroughly assessed the lunacy of earthly ventures, earthly dreams. (Between a man and a louse, what is there to get excited about?) Not only has size become ridiculous and meaningless but facts and figures as well, and striving even more. For unless one has glimpsed the hidden face of things every encounter begets illusion and disillusion. Thus, the line, as you will notice, begins nowhere and ends nowhere. It is not a faltering, groping line, but a premonitory one. (Why voyage further?) Like the historical line, it wanders. It can afford to wander. What it finds without seeking are the ruins . . . the ruins of thought, the ruins of love, the ruins of dream. But in the offing, like the mysterious voice of a fountain at night, comes the call of an antique land, the land of pure creation, where the nightingale makes light of human sorrow, human endeavor.

Foreword to
The Angel is My Watermark

PEOPLE OFTEN ASK, "If you had your life to live all over again would you do this or that?" Meaning — would you repeat the same mistakes? As for *les amours* I cannot answer, but as for *les aquarelles, oui!* One of the important things I learned in making watercolors was not to worry, not to care too much. I think it was Picasso who said, "Not every picture has to be a masterpiece." Precisely. To paint is the thing. To paint each day. Not to turn out masterpieces. Even the Creator, in making this world, had to learn this lesson. Certainly when he created Man he must have realized that he was in for a prolonged headache.

And Man, who also likes to play the Creator, discovers as he attains fulfillment, or a state of grace, if you like, that there is something beyond the mere act of creating. He comes to realize that it is not necessary to paint or describe in words what he sees around him. He learns to let things be. He discovers that simply by looking the world in the face everything he comes in contact with is a bit of a masterpiece. Why improve on it? Why make a fuss about it? Enjoy what you see, that's quite enough. The man who can do this is the accomplished artist. His creative merit lies in the ability to recognize and acknowledge that which has been created and which will elude forever his limited comprehension.

As for the rest of us, we who must sign our names to everything we do, we are simply apprentices. Sorcerers' apprentices. Though we pretend to be instructing others how to see, hear, taste, and feel, what we are really doing is to feed the ego. We are unable to remain anonymous, like those men who built the cathedrals. We want to see our names spelled out in neon lights. And we never refuse money for our efforts. Even when we have nothing more to say, we go on writing, painting, singing, dancing, always angling for the spotlight.

And here I come now with my watercolors beautifully reproduced in a handsome album—and my name in big letters. Another sinner. Another ego. I must confess it gives me great pleasure. I shan't be a hypocrite and say, "I hope it gives you pleasure too." The fact that after twenty years or so I have at last seen my dreams realized is all that matters. Frankly, I had hoped that maybe fifty or a hundred of my watercolors would be gathered together in one volume, instead of a mere dozen, but, as the saying goes, "better half a loaf than none."

The best part of it all is that I am not obliged to wait until I die. I can view them now *ici-bas*, with the eyes of a sinner, a wastrel, a profligate, rather than with the eyes of an angel or a ghost. That's something. Viewing them between the covers of a book, like so many museum pieces, I can take a posthumous look at them, as it were, and perhaps learn something of true humility.

The one thing I am certain of, now that my dream has been realized, is that I shall enjoy whatever I do henceforth more than I ever did before. I have no desire to become a masterful painter. As a matter of fact, the older I grow the less ambitious I become. I want simply to go on painting, to paint more and more, if not better and better, even though in doing so I may be commiting a sin against the Holy Ghost. One of the paradoxes of life is that the nearer one draws to the grave the more time one has to waste. Nothing has the grave importance it once had. Now I can lean heavily to right or left without danger of being capsized. I can wander off the course too, if I so desire, because my destination is no longer a fixed one. As those two delightful bums say time and again in *Waiting for Godot:*

"On y va?"

"Oui."

And neither budges.

I realize of course that these vagabond reflections and observations are hardly in the Teutonic tradition. They are not American either, if I know what I am talking about. But doesn't it make you feel good to read such nonsense? Suppose it's all cock-eyed, what I say—what difference? At least one knows where I stand. And you, my dear reader, are you standing on solid ground? Prove it!

Long ago—*il y a des siécles, il me semble*—when I was making merry writing *Black Spring,* I was already reveling in the fact that the world about me was going to pieces. Indeed from the time I was old enough to think for myself I was convinced of this. And then one day I came across Oswald Spengler. He confirmed my convictions. (And what a good time I had reading him, reading, that is, about "the decline of the West." It did me more good, honestly, than reading the *Bhagavad Gita*. It bucked me up.) Nor did I have the cheek then to say, as Rimbaud did, *"Moi, je suis intact!"* It didn't matter to me whether I was intact or falling to pieces. I was assisting at a spectacle: the crumbling of our civilization. Today the dissolution of our *Kultur* is proceeding even more rapidly, thanks to our improved technic and efficiency. One no longer needs to reach for a revolver — there are all kinds of lovely, instantaneous, wholly destructive playthings to choose from. Today everyone is writing about the approaching end, even our schoolchildren. Some of them seem to get a kick out of it too. But no one is any happier, have you noticed?

What I should like to recommend for the few remaining years, months or weeks that are left us is to piss the time away enjoyably. Making watercolors is one way. Try it, if you never have. No need to sign your name to them: nothing will be preserved, no matter whose name is signed. Turn them out one after the other, and don't worry about masterpieces. Nero fiddled while Rome burned. Making watercolors is much more fun. You won't harm anybody in doing so, you won't be making a spectacle of yourself, and you won't be collaborating with the enemy. (There is no enemy anyway, unless it is man himself.) When you retire for the night you will sleep more soundly. You may find your appetite improved too. You may even find yourself sinning with greater zest— enjoying it, what I mean.

What I am trying to say in my offhand way is that, come fair weather or foul, the ones who make the least fuss do more to save the world—how much is worth saving, do you ever stop to think?—than those who order us about in the vain belief that they have the answer to all our woes. When you put your mind to such a simple, innocent thing as the making of a watercolor you lose some of the anguish which derives from being a member of a world gone mad. Whether you paint flowers, stars, horses, or angels, you acquire respect and admiration for all the elements that go to make up our universe. You don't think of flowers as friends and stars enemies, of horses as Communists and angels Fascists. You accept them for what they are and you praise God that they are what they are. You stop trying to improve the world—or even yourself. You learn to see not what you want to see but what is. And what is is usually a thousand times better than what might be or ought to be. If we stop tampering with the world we might find it a far better place than we think it to be. After all, it's the only place. And whether it is to be ours for a few more weeks or a few more million years we will never get to know it, only to enjoy it, appreciate it, love it for what it is. In the end as in the beginning the word is—mystery. This mystery exists or thrives in every smallest particle of the universe. It has nothing to do with size or distance, with grandeur or remoteness. Everything hinges upon how you view the world.

With every work of art which is produced the same eternal question arises: "Is there more to what we see than meets the eye?" The answer, of course, is yes. In the humblest object we can find whatever it is we seek, be it beauty, truth, reality, divinity. The artist does not create these qualities, he discovers them, or uncovers them, in the process of doing. When he realizes the true nature of his role he can go on painting without danger of sinning, because he knows that to paint or not to paint amounts to the same thing. After all, one doesn't sing because one hopes to appear one day in an opera; one sings because one's lungs are full of joy. It's wonderful to listen to a great performance, but it's even more wonderful to encounter in the street a happy vagabond who can't stop singing any more than he can stop breathing. Nor does he expect any reward for his efforts. Efforts! The word has no meaning for him. No one can be paid to radiate joy.

So, whether the world is going to pieces or not, whether you are on the side of the angels or the devil himself, take life for what it is, have fun, spread joy and confusion.

REFLECTIONS ON THE DEATH OF MISHIMA

HENRY MILLER

1972

In a way there is no excuse for writing this article for the Japanese public. I am not an authority on Japan, nor have I ever visited the country, though I have been on the verge of doing so several times. It is true that I have a Japanese wife and that I have received many Japanese visitors here in my home. Several of my wife's friends have even lived with us for prolonged periods. It is also true that whenever I meet a Japanese, man or woman, I ply them with questions about Japan, her people, her customs, her problems. Add to all this that I am a devotee of the Japanese films, ranking the good ones above those of any other country. Further, I am more interested in Japan and her ways at the moment than in any other country of the world, except China. May I also add, very humbly that Zen interests me more than any other view or way of life.

The Japanese friends and visitors whom I meet are of all walks of life — writers, actors, film makers, engineers, architects, painters, singers, entertainers, business men, editors, art collectors and so on. They differ in their views and their behavior almost as much as would any cross-section of Europeans or Americans. Nevertheless there remains an aura of mystery, of impenetrability, surrounding the Japanese, both as a people and as individuals. I understand and sympathize with them up to a point — the women more than the men — and then

I am lost. I am never sure when the unexpected, the unpredictable will occur. Let me hasten to add that this does not make me uneasy, it intrigues me. I have always adored what is alien to me. I like to be stimulated, shocked, ast. unded.

And so, when I read of Mishima's dramatic demise I was filled with mingled feelings. I thought immediately of all the contradictions in his nature and at the same time I thought to myself — how very Japanese! Perhaps it is through the Japanese films that I became acquainted with, and am forever surprised, shocked and delighted by, the admixture in the Japanese of cruelty and tenderness, of violence and peacefulness, of beauty and ugliness. It is true, of course, that the Japanese are not alone in this respect. But in the Japanese, to my mind at least, this ambiguity exists more sharply and poignantly. In a way it accounts for their outstanding performance in all the arts, from poetry to painting to theatre. The aesthetic and emotional approach are always perfectly blended. A thing of horror can also be a thing of beauty: the monstrous and the aesthetic do not war, they complement each other as would two primary colors skillfully juxtaposed. A woman whose heart is broken, a Japanese woman I mean, a woman in utter despair and defeat, may yet exhibit a smile which only an angel of mercy could summon. Similarly, in the films dealing with the Samurai of old we are shown characters, masters usually, whose lives have been devoted to the sword and yet are able to demonstrate the utter futility of violence.

Youth, beauty, death — these are the themes which inform Mishima's writings. His obsessions, we might call them. Typical, one might say, of Western poets, or the Romantic ones at least. For this trinity he crucifies himself, a martyr just as surely as the early Christians.

He was a fanatic! That is the first and easiest charge that a Westerner finds to bring against him. But there are fanatics and fanatics. In the opinion of the world Hitler definitely was one. But then so was St. Paul. I have often thought of myself as possessing a fanatical strain: I would most certainly be afraid of assuming the powers of a dictator. Sometimes, pretending I possessed this total power, pretending that I was God, I have said to myself — "And what would you do to change the world to your liking?" With that I am paralyzed. I realize instantly that I would do nothing, that a repair job however prodigious has no relation to an act of creation.

No, I do not explain Mishima's suicide as a result of his fanaticism. If he was indeed determined, or obsessed, if you like, *for* what, *to* what did he dedicate his life? To the building of a beautiful body, to his art, to the restoration of the Samurai spirit? To all of these yes, but to his country, to Japan, first and foremost. He was a patriot in the strict sense of the word. He not only loved his country, he was prepared to sacrifice everything to save it.

It is said that he prepared for his sensational death months in advance. He had, indeed, lived with the thought of death, death by his own hand, for many years. It is further said of him that he wanted to die in the flower of life, while still beautiful, strong of body and at the height of his career. He did not want to die a dog's death, as so many of his compatriots do. And why not choose the time and manner of his own death? Did not the Greeks and Romans of old resort to suicide when they had had enough of the pleasures and sorrows of living? (Yet how different was the Roman fashion of slitting the wrists in a warm bath? Nothing dramatic, nothing sensational, about the performance. One might say they simply eased their way out of life.)

Fortunately for Mishima, he was able to blend all his notions about taking his own life with the higher one of thereby serving his country. It was the artist in him, no doubt, that decided how to make the best use of death. Horrible though his death was to many of us, and to his own countrymen alike, one cannot deny that there was a touch of nobility connected with it. One cannot say that it was the work of a madman or even of one temporarily deranged. Shocking as it was, it affected us in quite another way than Hemingway's suicide, performed by putting a shotgun to his mouth and blowing his brains out.

It is curious to reflect, since I have mentioned Hemingway's name, that Mishima should have so deliberately exposed himself to Western culture, Western thought, and yet die not only *in* traditional Japanese style but for the preservation of Japan's unique traditions. I do not believe that his concern was merely to restore the monarchy, nor even to recreate a Japanese army, but rather to awaken the Japanese people to the beauty and efficacy of their own traditional way of life. Who better than he, in Japan, could sense the dangers that menace Japan in following our Western ideas? By now it should be apparent to all the world, whether Fascist, Communist or Democrat, what poison is contained in our half-baked notions of progress, efficiency, security and so on. The price for all the seeming comforts and advancements proffered by the Western world is too great. The price is death, death not only in little ways but on a wholesale scale. The death of the individual, the death of the collective, the death of the entire planet — that is the promise hidden behind the flattering words of the exponents of progress.

Tradition, for us Americans, is a word of little moment. We have no tradition, unless it is that of the pioneer days. There are no frontiers any longer; our world grows daily smaller and smaller. There is room now only for pioneering spirits, and by that I do not mean Astronauts. The true pioneers are iconoclasts; it is they who preserve tradition, not those who struggle to maintain tradition and in doing so stifle us. Tradition can only truly express itself through the spirit of courage and defiance, not in outward observances and preservation of customs. I may be wrong, but I believe that it was in this sense that Mishima intended to restore the ways of his forbears. He wanted to restore dignity, self-respect, true brotherhood, self-reliance, love of nature not efficiency, love of country not chauvinism, the Emperor as symbol of leadership as opposed to a faceless, mindless herd obedient to changing ideological views whose values are established by political theorists.

I know that in speaking thus I appear to be white-washing Mishima. (I am aware of all the things he has been accused of.) But it is not my intention to white-wash Mishima, nor to condemn him either. I am not his judge. I speak thus because his death, the manner and purpose of it, caused me to question some of the things I valued or cherished, caused me, in brief, to reexamine my own conscience. When I question Mishima's ideas, his motives, his way of life or whatever, I question my own at the same time. I feel that it is high time the world in general questioned the values, the beliefs, the truths it holds. More than ever in the history of man do we need to ask ourselves — all of us, saints, sinners, beggars, law-makers, militarists — *where are we going?* Can we apply the brakes? Can we do an about face? Can we take stock of ourselves? Or is it too late?

One of my earliest heroes was the Filipino rebel Aguinaldo, who held out against the American military forces for years after Spain had surrendered. Like Ho Chi Minh, he was a real leader of his people. Another hero of mine was John Brown of Harper's Ferry fame, who boasted that had he a hundred men like himself he could defeat the U.S. Army, and I am inclined to think he could have done so. I would not call Aguinaldo a fanatic, but John Brown certainly was. His bold, rash, fantastic efforts to free the slaves accomplished wonders. Both Aguinaldo and John Brown had dedicated themselves to a great cause and, if their triumph was not an obvious one, it most certainly was a moral or spiritual one. Mishima's private little army has already disbanded, I understand, but Mishima's dramatic gesture, his defiance of the powers that be, may yet have far reaching results. "The end is not yet."

To my mind Mishima was too intelligent, or intellectual, too sensitive, too aesthetic, too Narcissistic, too much the artist to have been able to organize anything more than a mock or symbolic army. I cannot conceive of him retreating to mountain fastnesses to wage a prolonged guerilla war with the armed forces of his country. His concern, it seems to me, was not with an immediate victory over the opposing forces but with awakening his countrymen to the dangers that threaten them. Mishima was an extraordinary individualist but he was also a man of reason, of discernment, with a sense of human limitations. Just as he knew the power and the magic of words so he knew the dramatic and symbolic power of the act. He believed in himself, in his own powers, but not to the point of attempting the impossible.

To me the weakest aspect of his effort to restitute the

Japanese army was his failure to see that power corrupts, to realize that Japan, shorn of military power, succeeded in doing what few if any countries have been able to do without such assumed protection. Japan has prospered through her defeat, Germany also. At first blush it seems strange, almost incredible, yet it is quite simple. Not only did her military defeat bring the Japanese people to their senses, but through an imposed peace she has been able to do what her conquerors have failed to do. I will speak only of America in this connection. Look at this presumably all powerful nation! Does she not present a picture of disease, chaos, folly? Waging a senseless war against a small nation thousands of miles away — for what? To preserve the independence of a part of that nation, a people with whom we have no real ties or kinship? To protect our "interests" in Asia? To save face? To keep the world safe for democracy? Meanwhile, whatever our motives, our own country is falling apart: cities and states on the verge of bankruptcy, dissension widespread, funds lacking for educational purposes, millions living on the brink of starvation, racism rampant, alcohol and drugs vitiating the lives of young and old, crime ever on the increase, respect for law and order diminishing every day, pollution of our natural resources now at a frightening level, no leaders to look up to. . . . One could go on endlessly enumerating the evils which beset us. And yet we continue to pretend that our way of life is the best, that this democracy of ours is a gift to the world, and so on. How stupid, how absurd, how arrogant!

No, much as I believe the Japanese are entitled to have their own army and navy, their nuclear weapons, their own bombs, the complete arsenal of destruction, like any other nation, my fervent hope is that they will not succumb to this temptation. God forbid that the military take over, that once again they lead the Japanese people to slaughter. If there is to be an army, why not an army of peace emissaries, an army of strong, determined men and women who refuse to make war, who are not afraid to live defenseless, open and vulnerable? Why not an army that believes in the power of life, not death? Can we not have another type of hero than these obedient martyrs who kill and die for country, for honor, for this or that ideology, or for no reason at all? Japan is at a cross road. Soon she will be the second or third greatest power on earth. Can she continue to grow, to dominate world markets, to exceed the production of her competitors without the backing of a formidable military? *Can she conquer the world peacefully?* That is my question. It has never been done thus far. But it is possible.

Somewhere, in reading about Mishima, I came upon the phrase — "one pyrotechnical explosion: *death.*" In contrast to this we have the other kind of explosion: *Satori.* Between the two there is the difference between night and day, between ignorance and enlightenment, between sleep and waking. Despite all that Mishima has said about death, despite the fact that from the age of eighteen he nourished a romantic desire for self-extinction, Mishima also believed in being fully alive, awake in every pore and cell. To be fully aware, to awaken from the deep sleep in which we are buried, this was the goal of the Gnostics of old — and also of the Zen masters. *"Faites mourir la mort."*

It seems to be accepted nowadays more than ever that killing, individual and mass killing, is the order of the day. The horror of war seems to have faded; it is accepted as inevitable. The expression "cold war" seems to sum it up. One wonders what people with such an attitude hope to achieve. Victory? What kind of victory? If killing is the order of the day who then are the most excellent killers — those who kill the least (and win) or those who kill the most? Must the enemy be annihilated, or defeated and humiliated, or simply rendered *hors de combat*? And how are we to regard the leader who gives the order to press the button that releases the bomb which spares neither old nor young, crippled or insane, animals, crops, the earth itself? Is he a hero, a savior, a monster, a madman or an idiot? Is it necessary, now that we have made such progress technologically, to kill the innocent as well as the guilty? And if the enemy of today is to become the ally of tomorrow, what sense is there in wiping him out? Or, if he is merely defeated, beaten to his knees, why does the victor put him back on his feet again at the victor's own expense? We all know the answer to this riddle. We have to keep other people alive in order to keep our own people alive. *Business.* That is the heraldic emblem of the modern world. There is no logic to it whatever. It is a form of insanity, the insanity of civilization.

To look at it from another angle, is not the warrior a thing of the past, as useless and ridiculous as the dodo bird? When Mishima says, in *Sun and Steel,* that "the goal of my life was to acquire all the various attributes of the warrior", did he mean as "decoration"? We know that he admired the Samurai spirit and the cult of the sword, but of what use swords and all the chivalry of knighthood when there exists such a weapon as the bomb? We are no longer in the age when Richard the Lion-hearted, out of admiration for his opponent, invited Saladin to become a member of his own Order. Besides, talking of the sword and the various schools of the sword which existed in the days of the Samurai, what about the School of No Sword? Did Mishima not know of that? Even the Samurai, trained to kill as they were, living only to kill, so to speak, had come to realize that the best exposition of their skill lay in so living that they would never find themselves in the predicament of defending themselves by the sword. This attitude, in my mind, is a manifestation of the intelligent use of strength and skill in contrast to the heroic one of victory through death. Who wants victory, after all? Only stupid, cunning, mean spirits. What we all truly want is to stay alive as long as possible with all our wits and all our appetite for the enjoyment of life. We were not created heroes, poets, legislators, militarists, scholars, judges; we have created these divisions of activity through our particular way of looking at things, through our complicated way of life. Primitive man, who has outlived us thousands of times over, had no need for these diversifications. Neither have the wisest men in our midst. Though they are the Exemplars they never assume the leadership of a people. They do not seek to change the world, *they change worlds,* as St. Francis urged his too ardent disciples to do. In other words, they change their perspective and thus accept the world, which means understanding it, having compassion for one's fellow man, becoming brothers and not rivals or competitors, and certainly never judges.

I ask myself again and again — did Mishima really hope to change the behavior of his countrymen? I mean, did he ever seriously contemplate a fundamental change, a genuine emancipation? I am not questioning now the wisdom or the futility of his dramatic appeal through the use of dagger and sword. He who was endowed with high intelligence, did he not perceive the hopelessness of trying to alter the mind of the masses? So far no one has ever yet been able to accomplish this. Not Alexander the Great, nor Napoleon, nor the Buddha, nor Jesus, nor Socrates, nor Marcion, nor any one that I know of. The great mass of humanity slumbers, has been slumbering throughout all history, and will in all probability still be slumbering when the atom bomb takes its final toll. (Or do we need to await such a dramatic end? Are we not rapidly killing ourselves off in a thousand different ways, and with full knowledge of the end in sight?) No, one can shuffle the masses about like lumber, move them like pawns, whip them into a frenzy, order them to slaughter without let — especially in the name of justice — but one cannot awaken them, bid them live intelligently, peacefully, beautifully. There are and there always will be "the quick and the dead". And Jesus said — "Let the dead bury the dead."

His utter seriousness, it seems to me, stood in Mishima's way. I am tempted to say that this utter seriousness is a very Japanese trait. Only in the Zen masters do I find a true sense of humor. It is a sort of humor, I should add, that is also foreign to the Westerner. If we understood it, if we truly appreciated it, our world would collapse. The important thing is that this lack of humor leads to rigidity.

Even in the matter of developing his own body, which he did superbly, Mishima was dead serious and made it an end in itself. We have these body builders, these muscle men, here in America too. They strut about on the beaches like peacocks. They train their bodies to do extraordinary feats. They seem able at times to move mountains. But do they move any mountains? To what end this stunning musculature, this

Herculean strength, this god-like perfection? Is it to regard themselves in the mirror with pride and satisfaction? Is there not something feminine, something ridiculous about this cult of the body? As a boy I remember reading about the little band of Spartans who held the pass at Thermopylae until the last man died. There were illustrations in my story book of the Spartans before battle, combing and braiding their long hair. They looked beautiful and effeminate, heroes though they might be. The book spoke of the feeling of brotherhood which existed among men. I didn't know at the time the full implications of that word brotherhood. This kind of brotherhood nevertheless was of another order from the homosexuality practiced by the modern athlete and his ilk. It was a much wider, deeper form of love between man and man; it was practiced openly and communally, as was often the case with sister-and-brother religious groups that flourished at a much later date in Europe and even in America. With the Samurai of old it was doubtless the same. The buggery that goes on in modern armies, it goes without saying, is of another order. There is not even a hint of "melancholy splendor" about it.

If there was also something heroic about the Samurai and the Spartans and the Kamikaze fighters too, that kind of heroism has been preempted today by men in other fields than the military. Or so it seems to me. The world is less and less interested in men who undertake death missions. The conquest of the moon, for example, was a mission which demanded the brains and the cooperation of hundreds of men besides those who actually made the landing. It was an engineering feat first and foremost — a triumph of technology. I do not underestimate the valor of the Astronauts. But it should be noted, and it has been again and again, that they were what we call exceedingly "normal" individuals. They were not the heroic type. They followed instructions, a difficult feat in itself in this instance; they were not asked to die on the barricades, nor charge like the Light Brigade, nor commit voluntary suicide like the Kamikaze pilots. Their chances of succeeding were almost one hundred percent. And their achievements, as only time will tell, may possibly prove more important for mankind than the heroic sacrifices of all the heroes and martyrs who ever died for a cause or belief.

To come back to the subject of humor, or the lack of it. As I said at the beginning, I have not read all of Mishima's work, far from it. But thus far I have not detected a trace of humor in anything he wrote. I cannot, for some strange reason, help contrasting Mishima with Charles Dickens, whom Dostoievsky so admired though they were poles apart. What an eye-opener it was for me to stumble on G. K. Chesterton's book on Dickens just a few years ago and to discover the very great part which humor and pathos played in Dickens' work. Of course, no writer was better equipped than Chesterton to appreciate the humor of Dickens. Here is a passage from the end of the first chapter of this book:[*]

> "The fierce poet of the Middle Ages wrote, 'Abandon hope, all ye who enter here,' over the gates of the lower world. The emancipated poets of today have written it over the gates of this world. But if we are to understand the story which follows, we must erase that apocalyptic writing, if only for an hour. We must recreate the faith of our fathers, if only as an artistic atmosphere. If, then, you are a pessimist, in reading this story forego for a little the pleasures of pessimism. Dream for one mad

[*]*Charles Dickens,* by G. K. Chesteron; Methuen, Ltd. London

moment that the grass is green. Unlearn that sinis-
ter learning that you think so clear; deny that
deadly knowledge that you think you know. Sur-
render the very flower of your culture; give up the
very jewel of your pride; abandon hopelessness, all
ye who enter here."

How Zen-like, in many ways, is this appeal of Chesterton's! In a few lines he demolishes the props which
sustain our inadequate cultural view of the world. Back
to humanity. Common humanity. Throw away your
spectacles, your microscopes and telescopes, your national and religious differences, your lust for power,
your senseless ambitions. Get down on all fours and
teach the alphabet to the ants — if you can. Question
everything, but never lose your sense of humor. Life is
not a deadly serious affair, it is a tragi-comic drama.
You are the actor and the play itself. You are all there
is; there is nothing more nor anything less. So I interpret his words.

If one aims at affecting or moving the world, what
better way than to hold up the mirror so that we may
see ourselves as we really are, so that we may laugh at
ourselves *and* our problems. More effective than the
Samurai's sword or the short dagger for *seppuku* is that
Swiftian humor which stopped at nothing to make its
point. The man who could have made Hitler laugh
might have saved millions of lives. I mean it. The do-
gooders, whether they be saints or monsters, create
more ill than good. Louis Armstrong is a king, whereas
Billy Graham is only another preacher.

I know it is difficult to preserve a sense of humor in a
world which produces atom bombs like vegetables. But
if we had a stronger sense of humor perhaps there

would be no need to resort to that dolorous experiment of self-defense by mutual extinction. When, according to legend, Alexander the Great ordered a certain Indian sage to appear before him, when he threatened the sage with death should he refuse to obey, the sage gave a mighty horse laugh. "Kill *me?*" he exclaimed. "*I am indestructible.*" What an excellent sense of humor! A display not so much of courage as of certitude. And of a serene and supreme confidence in the power of life over death.

Was it his utter seriousness that led Mishima to feel that he had exhausted his powers at the age of forty-five, an age when many writers are only beginning to get their stride? What a misfortune to exhaust one's energies before one has really started! Of America a famous French writer (Duhamel) once wrote — "*Pourri avant d'être muri.*" A fruit, in other words, that rots before it ripens. Think, by contrast, of Hokusai, of Titian, of Michelangelo, of Picasso, and of that seemingly indestructible Pablo Casals.

I have met a number of Japanese writers in the last few years and I have been disagreeably impressed by the way they slave to earn a living, or to maintain a reputation. Whatever sense of play they may once have had seems lost, abandoned. I have a further impression that the whole body of workers in Japan are working like ants, killing themselves in this rat race which is called earning a living. Like the Germans, their counterpart, they seem to live only to work. And from being work slaves to dying like flies on the battlefield is only a step, an inevitable one. Should the workers of the world ever unite one wonders what the result will be — Utopia or mass suicide? The world of sports, a field in which the Japanese excel, is not an expression of the

play instinct but, like the industrial world, one of com-
petition, of breaking records, of pandering to the mob,
of making profits. The old Chinese sages who flew kites
to amuse themselves knew better, lived longer, laughed
harder and more frequently. They may not have had
enough muscle to kill a fly, but they did not end up
crippled or addlepated, nor were they concerned about
being remembered for their exploits after they were
dead.

PART II

The shock I experienced on learning of Mishima's
dramatic and gruesome end was reinforced by the recollection of a strange incident which happened to me
in Paris about thirty-five years ago. The incident I refer
to came to mind when, sitting in a doctor's office one
day, I happened to pick up a magazine (*Life*, I think)
in which there were photos of the decapitated heads of
Mishima and his comrade on the floor. Two things
struck me at once: one, the heads were not lying on
their sides but standing upright; two, one of the heads
bore a striking resemblance to my own which I had
once seen lying on the floor, but in pieces. Whether
real or imaginary, the resemblance between Mishima's
head and my own was frightening.

I had always imagined that if a head were severed
by the sword it would bounce and roll about on the
floor — but never land upright. Years ago I had read a

book called *Three Geishas** in which there was a story, purportedly a true story, called "Tsumakichi the Arm- less Beauty". It is a story which undoubtedly every Japanese is familiar with. In this story the patron of the school for Geishas returns from the theatre one night completely out of his mind and grabbing a huge sword proceeds to lop off the heads of the sleeping Maikos. Tsumakichi, who is sleeping downstairs, is awakened by the sound of the severed heads bouncing about like bowling balls. She awakens in terror to find her master standing above her with flashing sword. Before she can move he slashes off both her arms and disfigures her face. By a miracle she survives and eventually becomes one of the most famous geishas ever.

As for the resemblance between the two heads . . . About 1936 in the studio of a friend in the Villa Seurat, Paris, a young Jugoslavian woman, Radmila Djoukic, undertook to sculpt my head. The day she finished it — it was still in wet clay — a young Chinese student and myself were discussing English literature. He had men- tioned Shakespeare's name once or twice, which prompted me to ask if he had ever read *Hamlet*. He repeated the name questioningly, then exclaimed: "Oh yes, I remember now — you mean the novel by Jack London." I was so taken by surprise that I flung both arms in the air and inadvertently knocked the still moist head off the stand. To my utter dismay it fell to pieces — and not all the king's horses nor all the king's men could put poor Humpty Dumpty together again. Luckily however, a photo of the head had been taken the day before. Later this photo of the head was used as the cover of a dust jacket for my book called *Sunday After the War*. This head, which happened to be a very

---

Three Geishas, by Kikou Yamata: John Day Co., N.Y. 1956

true likeness in my mind, has always haunted me. Imagine my surprise and horror then in seeing it standing upright on the floor in company with that of an unknown head.

Though fleeting, the impression has never left me. From the moment of recognition to my encounter with Mishima in the afterworld was but a step. It was at this point that I interrupted my narrative to begin a dialogue with Mishima in limbo. My own imaginary death following close upon Mishima's it was as if our bodies were still warm and alive in every respect. It happens now that in my sleep I find myself continuing this dialogue with Mishima wherein we touch on things we might have discussed had we met in the flesh.

Several of these post-mortem themes Mishima himself touched upon in his *Confessions of a Mask.* "Can there be such a thing," he asks, "as love that has no basis whatsoever in sexual desire? Isn't that a clear and obvious absurdity?" Before giving answer I wish to quote these words from the same book: "To me Sonoko (the young girl he thought he was in love with) ap- my love of things of the spirit, of everlasting things." Let me say parenthetically that I hope never to forget these words in thinking of Mishima and his cruel fate.

To come back to his first question: can there be love without sexual desire? Let me supplement it with another which has been a subject of frequent discussion in this house: Can one go on loving some one if there is no response? To me the two questions seem to dovetail. They present the same seemingly impossible solution. Only freaks or superhuman beings would appear capable of answering such conundrums. By freaks I mean more specifically religious devotees who are not only able to live as gods, so to speak, but for whom such problems only fortify their character, their courage, their faith.

In the realm of love all things are possible. To the devout lover nothing is impossible. For him or her the important thing is — *to love*. Such individuals do not fall in love, they simply love. They do not ask to possess but to be possessed, possessed by love. When, as is sometimes the case, this love becomes universal, including man, beast, stone, even vermin, one begins to wonder if love may not be something which we ordinary mortals know but faintly.

Mishima's love of youth, beauty, death likewise seems to fall into a special category. It has no relation to the kind of love I have just described but, exaggerated as it was in his case, it is extremely uncommon. And it is tainted with Narcissism. To open most any one of his books one senses immediately the pattern of his life and his inevitable doom. He repeats the three motifs, youth, beauty, death, over and over again, like a musician. He gives us the feeling of being an exile here below. Obsessed by love of things of the spirit, everlasting things, how could he help but be an exile among us?

Who can possibly offer solace to the lonely exile? Only the great "'Comforter", interpret him as you will. But in Mishima's life there was no such "Comforter" apparently. He was not a man of faith but a man of principles. He was a Stoic in an age not of Hedonism but of stark materialism. He was revolted by the manner in which his countrymen seemed to wallow in their new-found freedom. Like the Westerners whom they emulated, their view of life had sunk to the level of the frog's. Gone the Apollonian and the Dionysian view of things. Money, comforts, security — these had become the goal. Could the cancer of modern life be extirpated? He obviously thought it could. But did he really think it through? How can the spirit of old, the saving virtues of our ancestors, possibly be grafted on to the worn-out, degenerate stock of modern man? To be sure, this so-called modern man has not really come into existence yet. The man of today is but a shadow of the modern man to come. He can neither go forwards nor backwards; he is stuck in the mire which his myopic vision of life has created. He is neither at home with himself nor the world which he is trying to dominate. His social instinct is atrophied, he lives isolate, fragmented, atomized and desolate.

Above everything, to the man of today life seems to have no meaning. It is often said that the prime phenomenon, or state of mind, is that of wonder. This too he has obviously lost. We try to explain the universe in terms of scientific theories, but we are unable to explain even the simplest phenomena. We overlook the fact that meaning comes only when we discover the purposelessness of creation. We mistake order and classification for explanation. We cannot abide the notion of disorder or chaos, yet the need for such an admission is essential. Likewise the need for utter nonsense. Only the genius seems to understand and appreciate the joy of sheer nonsense. Nonsense is the antidote to the monotony and emptiness created by our continual striving for order, *our order,* the antidote to our compulsive efforts to find meaning and purpose where there is none.

I have often wondered, in coming across the names of famous personages in European history mentioned by Mishima, who were his heroes? (I recall that as a child he adored Joan of Arc, until he discovered that she was a woman. He also mentions Gilles de Rais, that splendiforous and most enigmatic monster of the days of chivalry whose behavior puzzles us to this day.) Recently, as I lay in bed one night, I began to reel off the names of men whose deeds or thought or example seem to have had such influence upon our cultural life. And as I wrote them down I began arranging them in pairs in order to pose the question (to all and sundry) — If you had to choose, which of the two would you choose? Even if it be no more than a game the answers, it seemed to me, could provide some interesting revelations. In any case, it was Mishima I had in mind as I arranged the pairs. Which would *he* select, if he were obliged to make answer?

Laotse or St. Francis of Assisi
Leonardo da Vinci or Pico della Mirandola
Socrates or Montaigne
Hitler or Tamerlane
Alexander the Great or Napoleon
Lenin or Thomas Jefferson
Voltaire or Emerson
Joan of Arc or Mary Baker Eddy
Keats or Bashô
Rimbaud or Walt Whitman
Sigmund Freud or Paracelsus
Montezuma or Cortez
Pericles or Charlemagne
Karl Marx or Gurdjieff
Hokusai or Rembrandt
Richard the Lion-hearted or Saladin
Chuang-tsu or Rabelais

Unfortunately, because of ignorance, I have left out

the names of many famous Japanese whom Mishima
might have substituted for some of those given above.

There are so many things I wanted to discuss with
Mishima in our imaginary encounter in Devachan. First
of all, I would have made apology for my rudeness
upon meeting him in the flesh, in Germany, when he
was still a rather unknown figure. (I had completely forgotten that I had ever met him until the German and
Japanese newspapers disclosed the incident.) I would
have called for champagne and cigars — dream champagne, dream cigars, to be sure — but neither of us
would have known the difference. I would have en-
deavored to put him at ease, break down his guard,
make him laugh, if possible. Make him laugh heartily.
To do that alone would, in my mind, have made our
meeting worth while. (But how would I go about making him laugh? That thought tormented me.) Yes, I
would have engaged him in a fantastic conversation —
about angels Buddhist and otherwise, about the niceties
of language, about the absurdities of metaphysics,
about Zen in European literature, about love in the
Western world and love in the Eastern world, about
the physiology of love, that is to say, love among the
insects, love between germs and bacilli, love between
atoms and molecules, celestial love, perverted love,
Satanic love, fruitless love, love of the unborn, everlasting love and so on *ad infinitum*. I would have explained
to him that now, while waiting to be reborn, I would
have time to read *all* his books and perhaps to discuss
them with him, if he were so inclined. We would probe
everything except his personal problems. We would
have time to discuss Freud, Hegel, Marx, Blavatsky,
Ouspensky, Proust, Rimbaud, Nietzsche, whomever,
however. We might even take up the riddle of the

universe, both from Haeckel's standpoint and our own. We would summon houris and fairies, goddesses and supermen, space dwellers and astral bodies, heroes and monsters. "I promised to lead you to the ends of the world" — Alexander the Great to his war-weary soldiers. That's what I wanted to offer him. A trip, a real trip. A trip initiated by ideas, not drugs. A trip arm in arm through the Milky Way, with angels on either side of us as escorts. A journey through reality, not principles and ideas.

What a jolly idea! Nothing but time, or timelessness, on our hands. Putting off rebirth until it suited us, until we had decided the time and place for the next incarnation. Choosing our parents meticulously, and our new identities likewise. Choice again. Who would he like to be in the next incarnation — a leader of men or a simple fisherman? A hero or a nobody? As for myself, I had already thought it out before my demise. I would elect to be a nobody, anybody. Man or woman, no difference. A life of the senses, not the intellect. A common man, not a famous one. Someone you would pass in the crowd unnoticed.

But are we the arbiters of our fate? How I would like to have known Mishima's choice! I would be too discreet to press him on this point. Just as I would never dream of asking him what his marriage was like, or if he had ever hoped to find happiness in love, whether with a man, a woman, a chimpanzee or a cocoanut tree. More than anything I would have liked to know if he still thought it important to change the world — this world, the next world, or the world between worlds. That, and another question: *how had death tasted?* Was it truly the culmination of everything or did it still leave something to the imagination?

In the *Pavilion of the Golden Temple*, my dear Mishima, you used a phrase to describe an aspect of its beauty which I shall never forget. "You spoke of "adumbrations of nothingness". How it was in Japanese I shall never know, but in English there was magic in it. And somewhere else, in *Sun and Steel*, I think it was, you said you were beginning to plan a union of art and life. I wondered how seriously, how deeply, you had pondered that idea. I wondered if you had never sensed the contradiction implicit in that noble thought. You were always impaling yourself on the horns of a contradiction, were you not? Your whole life was a dilemma whose only solution was death. You made your own Gordian knot and you solved the problem by cutting it with the sword. Perhaps it was in that same book that you said your mind was forever beset by boredom. This, to me, is one of the strangest puzzlers I encountered in your work. You of all men confessing to boredom. Unthinkable. Was there nothing then that could truly satisfy you? Are you satisfied now, now that you accomplished, or failed to accomplish, your purpose? Have you come face to face with the Absolute? Do you believe there can be "a hero of enlightenment"? Or do you regard enlightenment as a myth invented by some crazy monk?

Yes, my dear Mishima, there are a thousand questions I would like to have put you, not because I think you have the answers now — when it is too late — but because the workings of your mind intrigue me. You worked so much, so hard, all your life — and to what end? Can you not give us another book, from the beyond, about the futility of work? Your countrymen need it; they are working like bees and ants. But are they enjoying the fruits of their labor, as the Creator intended them to? Do they look upon their work and find it good? You wanted to implant in them the virtues of their forbears, intending, I suppose, to thereby lend quality as well as substance to their lives. But what were the lives of your forbears, or mine for that matter, like? Have you ever studied the private lives of the millions of nobodies who do the work of the world? Do you think a man has a fuller, richer life because he is noble and virtuous? Who is to be the judge in these matters? Socrates had one answer, Jesus another. And before them was Gautama the Buddha. Did he have the answer? Or was his answer silence?

I am sure silence is the one thing you came at last to appreciate. You tried so hard to say everything, and then to do everything. You were prodigious in your Protean exploits. The only thing you omitted in your turbulent career was to be a clown. You wrote of angels but you overlooked their counterpart, the clown. They are of the same breed, only one is celestial and the other earthly. A hundred thousand years from now, when we shall have conquered space — whatever that may mean — we shall probably be communicating with the angels. That is to say, those among us who no longer place such emphasis upon the physical body, those who have learned to use their astral body. The men, in other words, who have discovered that all is Mind, that what we think is what we are and what we have is what we truly want. Even in that distant day there may still exist two worlds — the hell the world has always been and the world of free spirits who know that the world is of their own making. In his oration On Human Dignity Pico della Mirandola said:

"In the midst of the world, said the Creator to Adam, I have placed thee, so that thou couldst

*look around so much easier and see all that is in
it. I created thee as a being neither celestial nor
earthly, neither mortal nor immortal alone, so that
thou shouldst be thy own free moulder and over-
comer; thou canst degenerate to animal, and
through thyself be reborn to godlike existence. . . .
Thou alone hast power to develop and grow
according to free will; in one word, thou hast the
seeds of all-embracing life in thyself!"*

Our ancestors have made many experiments, of
which yours must seem even to you to be but a trifling
one. Even in earlier times we have had men who were
five or ten thousand years ahead of their time. And if
we could go back far enough we would undoubtedly
discover that women too once ruled the world, once
dreamed of putting an end to earthly sorrow and
misery. (Ironically, only primitive man has succeeded
in adapting himself to his environment and continuing
his most ancient way of life with relative ease.) In the
dim mist of the past names and deeds have been forgotten by us who think that the problems which con-
front the world today are novel and overwhelming.
Times washes all things away, the good and the bad
equally. Life continues like a never-ending stream,
piling up more and more debris which we fatuously call
history. What is history but a fiction which lulls us to
sleep or sharpens our fears? Are we a part of history or
is history a part of us? In five thousand, or ten thousand
years, Japan may be no more. She may die of inanition
or go down in a glorious clash of arms. Who knows
what her end will be like? We can foresee nothing,
niether our doom nor our salvation.

The little army you created, your élite corps, so to
speak, will probably not even be remembered a hundred years from now. Your name may live on, not as

another would-be saviour of your country but as an entertainer, as a spinner of words. You may be remembered as a lover of beauty whose words provoked a mild ripple of excitement. Words and deeds live separate lives. Words may touch the spirit, but only spirit answers to spirit. As for deeds, they are as dust. The ruins of ancient splendors lie all about us; they do not inspire us to nobler, more grandiose efforts.

I am as guilty as you, my dear Mishima, in trying to make the world a better place to live in. Or at least I began with that hope. In some peculiar way the practise of writing taught me the futility of such a pursuit. Even before I had read St. Francis' words of wisdom I had made the decision to look upon the world with different eyes, to accept it as it is and be content to make my own world. This about face did not blind me to the evils which exist, nor make me indifferent to the suffering and misery which men endure. Neither has it made me less critical of the laws, the institutions, the codes of behavior which we continue to live by. It is hard, indeed, for me to imagine a world more absurd, more unreal, than the one we are now living in. It seems, as the Gnostics of old put it, more like "a cosmic mistake", more like the work of a phony Creator. For the world to become livable there would need to be what Nietzsche called "a transvaluation of values". To put it mildly, it is an insane world in which, alas, the insane are outside the asylum and not inside. In short, so it looks when one would like to have things his own way. Japan is no more crazy, no more sane, than the rest of the world. She has her zombies just as Haiti does; she has her war lords just as Germany does; she has her ruthless industrial magnates just as America does. She has her men of genius also, neither greater nor lesser than those of other countries. Her problems are not unique, nor the solution to them either. She was your world, your conditioner, just as America is mine.

Perhaps I delude myself, but I feel that I have found my own private insane asylum. I too may be crazy, but in a different way from my compatriots. I no longer mind watching my fellow citizens march to their own destruction, if that is what they wish to do. That is their funeral, not mine. What obstacles they put in my path I have learned to live with, but these obstacles are becoming less and less frightening, less and less inhibiting, as time goes on. One learns to play the game — not by observing the rules but by circumventing them. There is no school in which to learn the art unless it be life itself. Only a seeming mastery can ever be achieved. In the end we all get fucked, each and every one of us, including those who fought for their country and those who did not.

Eventually cemeteries have to make way for farms and habitations of the living. If only the dead could talk — not about the afterworld but about the one they departed! If only we were able to learn from the experience of others! But we do not learn that way, if indeed we learn at all during our short stay here below. All we can hope to learn is how to live, but for that there are no instructors. Each one has to find out for himself, or as some say, find the Path and become one with it. The irony of it all is that the errors one makes are just as important, or perhaps more important, than the right findings. Trial and error, trial and error — until one gives up trying, which is simply another way of saying gives up butting his head against a stone wall.

From the moment the soldier goes into battle his one obsessive dream is of peace. Perhaps the generals and admirals dream of victory, but not the men who do the fighting. Judging from what I have read of you, my dear Mishima, this subject of peace does not seem to occupy a great place in your work. I thought about this when reading of your little band of well-tailored soldiers. (Forgive the tinge of mockery.) Every time I see a well-trained army marching off to war I think of how those spic and span outfits, those polished boots and polished buttons will look after the first encounter with the enemy. I think of how those millions of bright uniforms are destined to become nothing more than ragged, filthy shrouds covering dead and mutilated bodies. Strange, the importance given the uniform. As if the body were leased for the lifetime of the uniform. When forming your little army I wonder if you ever gave a thought to the possible finish of those uniforms which cost you so much time and effort to pay for.

This may seem a nonsensical consideration in view of your high purpose, but surely the man of action whose role you were presuming to play must have realized that there are such things as mud, blood, shit and vermin which enter into the game of making war. Indeed, to speak only of the first and last mentioned items, they play a major part in every war. But perhaps the aesthete and the dandy in you forbade such considerations.

Today the whole "civilized" world is nothing more than an armed camp in which the victims are silently screaming "Peace, Peace, give us Peace!" And you, my dear Mishima, seem to have been strangely unconcerned. Did you take it for granted that once you had made your ploy everything would proceed smoothly? Or were you simply oblivious of the consequences of rearming? Was it enough to confess failure and atone for it by honorable *seppuku*? I can't believe that you were quite that immune, quite that much of a solipsist. This, of course, is a subject I would dearly have liked to discuss with you in limbo. All that is left us now is conjecture. Some will find satisfaction in calling you a fool, others in calling you a fanatic, and still others in branding you a hero.

Whatever you were your absence is a loss to the world. So we are inclined to say when a man of genius passes from among us. Actually, there is nobody, nothing, which can be fitted into that cliché "a great loss to the world". Think of the millions and millions slaughtered in war alone, to say nothing of earthquakes, tidal waves, plagues and so on. When the death toll is finally reckoned the loss of a few distinguished individuals is solemnly proclaimed. The generals lost in combat usually receive undue notice. But it is not they who constitute the great loss to society. They are the supposed heroes whose duty it is to risk death on the battlefield. No, it is the artists and thinkers whose loss we bemoan. Generals and admirals can be made any time, any place, but not creative individuals. Usually it is too late when the words and deeds of the creative ones receive attention; we make do by adding their names to the illustrious dead already embalmed in the pantheons of the world.

But what of the countless millions who died or were maimed and broken in spirit? Were there not some among them destined to be even greater than those already enshrined? Were there not quite possibly some thinkers and inventors, some men of more than ordinary vision who, if they had lived, might have transformed our world? Think of the tremendous changes wrought by men like Edison, Marconi, Einstein, to mention but three. Surely not all the unknown, not all the forgotten men who died in battle were dolts and idiots. Does the world miss them, does it mourn their loss? The world has not time for such speculations. *Avanti! Avanti!* it yells. *Forwards!* even though forwards sometimes means backwards. *Forwards!* even though it mean universal destruction. Life, they say, life demands it. But whether it be life or death that pushes us on the world manages somehow to survive. Maybe not my world or your world, but "the world". One wonders sometimes what that strange word "world" really means.

Now that you are no longer of it, rest in peace!

Little Thoughts En Route —
      on Greece, on the Greeks,
and on other things.
      For his most sensitive
majesty, King George Seferis
of Smyrna!
      His obedient servant,

                  Henry Miller

                        November 1939

"Et bon voyage à tout le
monde!"

First
Impressions
of Greece

Henry Miller

1973

Begun at Hydra, at the home of Ghika. Surrounded by Madame Hadji-Kyriaco, Katsimbalis, Aspasia, Seferiades, and the chamber maids. Ripe, fecundating atmosphere—for conversation, dream, work, leisure, indolence, friendship and everything. Everywhere the ancestral spirit. The whiskey excellent, especially favorable for discussions about Blavatsky and Tibet.

ISLAND OF HYDRA — 11/5/39

The birth-place of the immaculate conception. An island built by a race of artists. Everything miraculously produced out of nothingness. Each house related to the other, as though by an unseen architect. Everything white as snow and yet colorful. The whole town is like a dream creation: a dream born out of a rock. At every step of the way the picture changes. The whole island is like a rock built on a revolving stage. Even the climate revolves. We are going backwards towards the summer solstice. Winter will come with roses, melons, grapes. The soil is like dried blood, a red which becomes Pompeiian as it climbs the walls. The islands float on bands of light, fastened down only by tiny white shrines which are again like dream visions. The town, which has organically grown out of the rock in artistic formation, seems to be born anew every day. It is like Holland or Denmark, except that it is Greek.

In the fortress where Ghika lives the discussion always seems to revolve about Byzance. Byzance is the cultural link. But the pendulum swings back and forth—from Mycenae to Periclean Greece, from Minoan times to the revolution, from Hermes Trismegistus to Pericles Yanopoulos or Palamas or Sekelianos. The meals are Gargantuan—the hors d'oeuvres alone suffice. Then the desserts—melon, figs, green oranges, grapes, walnuts, Turkish pastry, which is not really Turkish but Greek—*Byzantine*—and the retzina which dissolves everything in gold dust and aerates the lungs by a sort of refined turpentine shellac which evaporates and creates well-being, joy, conversation. Every anecdote uncovers another Greek phenomenon—the human phenomenon—who vies with the natural wonders here in variety and eccentricity. (The story of the banker who wrote bad verse. The imbecile who kept a 33-volume pornographic diary. The nymphomaniac who danced naked on the estate and seduced the guests. Etc, etc. Legends, fables, myths galore.)

The road to the sea, amidst cemeteries of gray stones, gray heather, lavender-green rock, bloody soil, with white everywhere and blue and walls dripping with ochre. The astounding faces of the children, all so different. Some like Africans, some like vase figurines (?), some like coffin portraits. The maid who is called, who is *baptized*, Demeter! The admiral's house. The destruction of the Turkish Armada. Everything is legendary, fabulous, incredible, miraculous—yet true. Everything begins and ends here.

To Spetsai with Katsimbalis by one of the innumerable discarded ferry-boats which the Greeks buy as old junk and continue to sail for twenty or thirty more years, breathing life into the boats by their courage, tenacity and skill. At Hermione, on the Peloponnesus, we get off the boat absent-mindedly. Only when we stand before the war memorial does Katsimbalis suddenly realize his error. A mad dash in a broken-down Ford to the sea. My first view of Argolis, of a land which excites me immediately. Perhaps this is the very oldest part of Greece. It seems so. It has a primeval quality, a stillness which is enchanting—and healing. Argolis is close to me, the most intimate soil I have yet seen in all my wanderings. To ride through this landscape in the battered Ford is incongruous. All invention now seems childish, more than ever so. Greece will outlive all ideas of "Progress", assimilate, destroy, recreate everything which now seems essential to life. Here is where the buttons go back to the buttonmoulder, where everything is "refunded", in the mystic sense.

At the seaport a violent storm. Finally the sky clears and in a swollen sea we set forth for Spetsai in a benzina. Hardly have we put out to sea when another trim little boat appears. We race side by side, the tiny craft bucking like broncos. For me it is a Homeric voyage. The boat has become a mythological animal. With a stiff wind blowing, rocks to either side, huge waves threatening to swallow us if we ride into the trough of the waves, the man at the tiller nevertheless leaves the helm to take down the tarpaulin over our heads. An act of sheer recklessness in order to gain time, to save a little fuel. We watch him breathlessly, not daring to say a word. A Greek act—the daring which always accompanies the ruse. This is what distinguishes the heroic Greeks from the Vikings. Both indomitable, sure, reckless, the greatest navigators in the world. But with the Greek I feel absolutely safe. His daring is always based on certitude. He has genius when he undertakes a dangerous task. And what a hard school of training the Mediterranean offers! Who graduates from this school is a master mariner, capable of sailing any sea.

Spetsai seems pale by comparison with Hydra. Seems anomalous, soft, heterogeneous. It has its own charm, however. Marooned there for four days we explore the island on foot. The atmosphere is even more redolent of the past than Hydra. It is somewhat sad. Especially forlorn at the old port, where boats are still being built and seamed and caulked. Four sailboats lined up in mid-harbor, riding at anchor—like so many scenes out of French paintings. But something peculiarly sullen, something almost un-Greek about the atmosphere. The four boats nestled in the hollow of the hill stick in my memory. It is like the twilight of forgotten deeds. Things are dying silently, hidden away from the public eye.

In Bubulina's home, the place where she was shot. Katsimbalis recounting her exploits. Here lives Mr. Tsatsos, professor at the University of Athens, now in exile and sleeping in this lugubrious, ghost-ridden house. Below is a little shrine, and when one goes to the toilet one is pervaded by fumes of incense. The huge room where Bubulina died now filled with beds and bedsprings, and beneath the flooring the sound of rats scampering madly.

Tsatsos I envy. I congratulate him on his being exiled. I glance at his books. Goethe, Sheridan, Dante, Aristotle, D. H. Lawrence, Homer etc. Over his bed a huge mosquito net. He will remember this place later. He will think how fortunate he was to have passed these months of solitude here. I congratulate him again now—I wish him well.

There is also John Stefanakos, a Greek from Buffalo, N.Y. Fifteen years in America have made him more American than I shall ever be. Even his accent is more American than mine. John has become a sow—a fat sow with gravy dripping from his lips. He has nothing to do but lend money at interest to his compatriots. He has a house which is like a refined lunatic asylum. His wife is a mental but agreeable defective. She is also handy with the needle, a virtue which John appreciates. But John's heart is in Buffalo, at the race track there. He has brought back with him enough clothes to last him the rest of his life. He has seen nothing of Greece, except Spetsai where he was born. He thinks Greece needs more machinery, more money. He is a perfect specimen of the lost man, the man whom America takes to her bosom, castrates and fattens like a eunuch. He knows how to smoke expensive cigars, drink whiskey, talk out of the corner of his mouth, etc. He has been drained of everything necessary to make a human being. He is like a discarded tin can such as one sees on the shores of every country in the world, in the wake of modern progress. He and Bubulina are two totally different animals. Long live Bubulina!

One day some enterprising Anglo-Saxon will write a comparative study of Bubulina and Jeanne d'Arc. He will omit the fucking business, naturally. It is necessary to say a word here parenthetically. Every female heroine, every female saint was endowed with tremendous sexual ardor. Bubulina fucked her way to fame. She died *enceinte*. (For further details, address George Katsimbalis, Amaroussion.) I pass on. Pass to the white, still nunnery on the hill overlooking the two arms of the sea. An all-pervading peace and quiet here. On the terraced slopes some old nuns at work with pick and spade. The birds singing in their cages suspended from the grape arbor that shelters their white little cells. Again it comes over me strongly that it requires high intelligence to select such a life as these old nuns have chosen. All that they voluntarily relinquish to come here they regain a thousand-fold. The belief, the morality, the ethic are nothing—it's the *form* of the life which gives peace and character and wisdom.

Spetsai marks an important step in the longer journey I am making. My long walks by the sea with Tsatsos brought deep corroborations of the answers I had already given to certain inner problems. Though antipodal to one another, we understood each other perfectly, in spite too of the language problem. What was vitally important, chez Tsatsos, was his purity. I felt that I had met a man of fine spirit, that he was a link with those others past and future whom it is in my destiny to meet. Some give courage, others confirmation. It was too bad my friend "Alf" was not there to listen in on Goethe. To find a Greek talking this language, talking "religiousness", was a great surprise. And I believe Tstatsos too was surprised, in his fashion. (But the greatest surprise was John of Spetsai listening to "Mister George", as he quaintly called Katsimbalis. It was all Greek to him, as we say in America.) Race, language, milieu, profession, métier, education—what do these things signify when the spirit is altered? Strange links, strange dissociations. There are only men, only individuals, everywhere. The rest is a foolish, meaningless babble between great convulsions of time and matter. The Anargyrios, for example—a colossal mistake, an illusion on the part of a man who had no illusions. Teaching the Greeks "team work", as the naif English professor put it—a piece of sheer fatuity. Futile to the nth degree. When the Greeks adopt the harness they will cease to be Greek. But only the English with their innate insensitivity to what is other, different, could believe in such nonsense. Anargyros continues the American millionaire tradition of doing what one pleases in this life and trying to undo his work in the next life, by endowments. All public endowments are bad, in Greece as everywhere else. The spirit of Anargyros is in his Helmar, Murad and Turkish Trophies cigarettes, which I am going to smoke once again when I am rich enough to afford the luxury. (The first cigarette I ever smoked was one of the Anargyros variety. America has lost its taste for them now. To all Greeks I say: "Smoke a Murad!")

Another discarded rolling tub, an English channel boat, taking us to Nauplia. We are to put in at Leonidion on the way. The sun is setting. Katsimbalis is talking. Marvellous talk, one story after another, one better than the other, a ceaseless outpouring as the darkness comes on. I am curious to see the ancestral spot. I had already formed an image of it in my mind. We come close to shore. It is precisely as he had described it. A sort of Dantesque pass in the black-green bone of the mountain range. The foothills open up slowly, like heavy drapes drawn aside by giant hands on noiseless pulleys. The village, like a handful of chicken feed, nestles in the harbor. One strong electric light gleams from the shore. A cold dank icy breath blows upon us. A boatload of chairs is being rowed out. They look incongruous. Are there people sitting in chairs here in this chill marsh vapor? Where are the eagles, the vultures, the condors? Where are the Indians? Somehow I expect to see Indians stepping out of their shadowed wigwams. The place is a monumental horror, a living symbol of dread and foreboding. We go back in. We drowse a bit. We awake. We are in Paris—on the Rue du Faubourg Montmartre. Katsimbalis does not know yet what this street means to me, how I too have haunted it night after night. I let him talk. I am stupefied by the rich unending flow. What *warm* stories! How full, how human, how dark, tender, loving, generous. He is not a *raconteur*. He is a living organ, a voice pealing heavy sonorous notes which reverberate in the immense solitude of a deafened Greece. He is bestowing on me, a stranger, great gifts, great linguistic bouquets studded with live flesh. I feel as though I may suddenly bifurcate and no longer tell my own story but his. I am afraid to listen too well—the responsibility is too great. . . . As we arrive in port two prisoners stand handcuffed together. I see Katsimbalis and myself handcuffed too, but not by law. I feel that we are handcuffed for eternity. We will travel the road together. I salute my brother in crime.

A brief walk through the town before retiring for the night. Nauplia has a somewhat French appearance. It is a distinctive town, an ordered place. The little square in front of the museum, where the crazed inhabitants walk up and down, breathes an atmosphere. The fortress looms above. The silence weighs oppressively. It is dead silent. The streets lead out, into open geometric space. The statue of a hero stands naked, shivering, bleak, wan, forlorn in the vast night. The statue is a piece of insanity. In the morning I shall see the plain of Argos, the smoke rising gently from the imaginary wigwams. A land opposite us such as William Penn saw when he greeted the Delawares. The Indians are haunting me ever since I caught sight of the Peloponnesus. It is an enigma. I leave it as such. . .

Awake at dawn, shivering with the cold. Stroll down to the quay and look at the mist rising from the low plain opposite. I am facing Argos. I get a shock. I only now recall *what* Argos means—the myths and legends. Suddenly I see why it looked so familiar to me. It is a replica of the photographic plate in my history book at school. In the early morning mist it is even more North American. Where are the buffalo, the canoes, the wigwams? I sit in the salon waiting for Katsimbalis. I read all the letters which the clients have written for the enterprising manager of the Grande Bretagne. They were all written by half-wits. I would like to write a good one about the Trojan Horse, but the hotel is to be torn down soon. . . .

A ride in the automotrice, for 12 drax (!!) to Mycenae. We are walking the road from the station on a Sunday morning—not quite 8 a.m. A boy is crying bitterly because his comrade has taken all his money away. It is grotesque to hear this weeping so early in the morning. He is like a lost animal. As we curve round the last bend I notice a round smooth green tumulus—the most perfect stretch of green I have ever seen. I feel sure the dead are sleeping beneath this huge pillow of earth. A few steps farther on we pass the first tomb—Agamemnon's. Now I catch sight of Mycenae, the ruins, the place of horrors. Like Tiryñs, it is again well chosen. Tiryñs, Argos, Mycenae—three strategic and sacred spots. Nothing will ever destroy the validity of these sites. Civilizations may come and go, but these places will remain intact. They are eternally rooted in the landscape, in time, in history, in the evolution of the human race.

A most important item: lunch al fresco at the Belle Hélène! The best meal I have had in Greece thus far. And a fat book on archaeology by the British school as an hors d'oeuvre. Dozing off under the tree. A group of men in the field measuring the land—a dispute about property. Somehow this scene strikes me as most appropriate. It touches me. Suddenly the earth has become important again— even a square yard of it. Far from megalopolitan worries. No abstract discussions, no abstract reckoning, no abstract holdings.

Land, land, measured out by a tape measure. Quite thrilling. Still more thrilling to think that the fellow who owns it will till the soil indifferent to the dead relics which are strewn about. The eternal peasant, living in the eternal present. The man without history, the bottom man who supports the cultural flux. . .

At Epidauros. Perhaps *the* most perfect spot of earth I have yet seen. The day is superlatively fair, the blue sky even more electric than usual, the hills cutting the sky with a razor's edge. So this was one of the great therapeutic centers of the ancient world! Even if there were not a stone left to testify to its glory one could reproduce it imaginatively. I think of my psychoanalyst friends—Otto Rank, Dr. René Allendy, Dr. E. Graham Howe, I think of Jung, Freud, Stekel et alia. They are working only with the débris of humanity, with hulks and remnants, with torsos and decapitated heads.

In Aesculapian times man was still a whole being. He could be reached through the spirit. Body and spirit were one. Metaphysics was the key, the can-opener of the soul. To-day not even the greatest analyst can restore to men what they have lost. Each year there ought to be a congress of physicians meeting at Epidauros. First the medicos should be cured! And this is the place for the cure. I would give them first a month of complete silence, of total relaxation. I would order them to stop thinking, stop talking. Stop theorizing. I would let the sun, the light, the heat, the stillness work its havoc. I would let them become slightly deranged by the weird solitude. I would order them to listen to the birds, or the tinkle of goat bells, or the rustle of leaves. I would make them sit in the huge theatre and meditate—not on disease and its prevention but on health which is every man's prerogative. I would forbid cigars, the heavy black cigars of the Freudian school, and above all books. I would recommend the cultivation of a state of supreme and blissful ignorance. I would give them each a string of beads, gratis. And grapes warm with sunshine. Then I would have a shepherd come and blow a few wild Anatolian notes on a broken flute. . .

Visit to Daphni. The church interests me far less than the landscape, the light, the lavender gray rock. I start walking along the Sacred Way towards the sea. As on another day when unwittingly I walked to Byron, I am intoxicated by the atmospheric conditions. Today, Sunday, I have seen the miraculous phenomenon of light inhabiting trees. The light literally rushes through the foliage, creating a green vaporous shroud, an indwelling halo, the aura of the tree itself. The soul of the tree stands revealed. The trees are bathed in holiness, in the purity of their own essence. The separation between body and soul is acutely distinct. It is maddening. The more so because of the austerity of the soil, the rosy gray, the slightly Tibetan cast of the slopes. There are no longer leaves, there are only intoxicated green brushstrokes waving with the wind. The sagebrush is silvery and hugs the earth tenaciously, as if guarding deep reptilian secrets. I start to climb a hillside to get a better view of the landscape, but I am too frightened by the naked beauty. I stand half-way up the slope looking about me uncomprehendingly. It is like one of the mad magical scenes which Shakespeare now and then, in his great despair, conjured up. Here man joins up with the reptilian world. Here he dare not walk erect, except as a god. This is the punishment inflicted throughout the ages, the great secret of the sway of Greece, of her temporary abnegation or abdication. Man had first learned here how to walk as a god. He will walk again one day—as a god. When he has forgotten what he now knows. (To-day, my first day in a flying machine, the thought came to me—how utterly ridiculous, how degrading, to be sitting in a chair in the air, propelled by a motor, and oneself utterly passive, utterly useless. Flying is the lowest form of voyaging. One might just as well be a lump of shit.)

———

In Heraklion—freezing to death. The banana trees are on the other side of the island. Winter is here, but there are no fires. We

wait for the sun to come up. I think of the dead cat lying head first
in the deep gulch beyond the walls of the town. This morning the
flies were feasting on its carcass. To-night the flies are probably
dead. Heraklion too is dead. It is like Imperial City, California,
where I became definitely schizophrenic. I feel that I am in the
Azores, at Madeira, though the architecture is à la Dickens of *The
Old Curiosity Shop*. I stop and listen to a phonograph on a chair in
the middle of the street in front of a restaurant. It sounds Turkish.
The people are looking at me because I am listening to the phonograph. Everybody has a Cyrano de Bergerac physiognomy. The
bakery shops are thoroughly Pompeiian—so are the butchers'
blocks. An added touch is the butcher's blood-red apron, like a
Venetian sail. In the charming courtyards are beautiful faces—
startlingly beautiful girls, marooned here for life. The men walk
about like pirates on a holiday. The tailors sit on their bench
without shoes. Boots everywhere, of the finest kid. The red ones
particularly fascinating. The food is abominable. If it weren't for
Bill X—, owner of the Café Central, I would die of ennui. He
regales me about Montreal, where he owned a flourishing restaurant until the crisis cleaned him out. Bill eats early, contrary to
Greek law. He says he means everything he says—not like his
compatriots. They have no sense of business, he says. They only
like to play tricks on one another. When he transformed the café
they thought he was crazy. He had good drinking water, which he
brings from another village. He is a white man.

Suddenly, seeing his portrait for the ten thousandth time, I
realize that Metaxas is the dead image of Otto Rank, the
Viennese psychoanalyst. They should put a cigar in his mouth to
complete the resemblance. Nice too to see Laurel and Hardy
advertised at the cinema. And Arizona Shoe Polish. The world is
progressing. The Minoans had to do without these luxuries. Poor
devils, what reminds me terribly of New York, of the ghetto, the
slums, are the perennial kiosks littered with shoelaces, cigarettes,
candy, junk. The same wretched faces peering out at me from the

little cabins in which these poor devils pass their lives in solitary confinement. I see them looking at my coat, my hat, my shoes. Every American *must* be a millionaire. And yet, if we were to compare notes, compare bank accounts, property, holdings, possessions, I am poorer than any of them. What we see in these wretched faces peering out of the kiosks is *despair*. In this sense all Americans are millionaires. Every American has hope. He will not pass his life sitting in a kiosk. He may punch tickets in the subway, but he doesn't sell shoelaces, etc. That is reserved for "immigrants".

And, when I arrive at Phaestos, at the top of the world, at the one place on earth which is nearest to heaven, there stands Kyrios Alexandros, bowing and kowtowing at 100 yards' distance. "God has sent you!" he says, in greeting.

I am the first visitor, the first tourist, in several months. Alexandros weeps, kisses my hand, calls me Mister Professor. *Bon! D'accord.* What is there to eat? Fortunately I have brought a few provisions along. While Alexandros scrapes the mud off my shoes I ask about the larder. It is empty, alas. But—he has the black wine which Bill X—from Montreal recommended me to try. Good. Before looking at the ruins I decide to eat. I ask Alexandros to share the meal with me. He seems positively frightened by the suggestion. It is not done. *Soit.* I begin sipping the wine. The olives are lousy—without taste, unless it be the taste of mud. Alexandros talks. He is wringing his hands and calling on God to put a stop to Herr Hitler so that there may be tourists once again. I am thinking of a thousand things at once—of the women who walked about the palace in winter, of Arizona and New Mexico, of the Valley of the Moon in California, of Shangri-la, because this is the closest we'll ever get on this earth to the Shangri-la of the cinema. Most of all I feel the lack of a companion. The site is so marvellous, my well-being so complete, that suddenly I feel guilty, guilty as a criminal, for enjoying all this alone. On the side looking towards Mt. Ida the autumn colors of the earth are ravishing. For the first time in my life I see a symphony of umbers. And towards the sea that red earth, the primordial clay out of which man was formed in God's image. Man has woefully fallen from his state of grace, but nature remains eternally holy. The brown slopes are like the skin of water animals. They have been washed through aeons of time with alluvial deposits. They have been scorched, baked, blistered, and then deluged with torrents. Everywhere the caress, everything softened down, subdued, sweetened. It is the softest spot of earth I know of. It is feminine through and through. I feel certain the site was chosen by the dynastic queens of Minos. It is the female line of the great dynasty which has given to the land-scape its character, its charm, its subtlety—and its inexhaustible variety.

Knossus I tried to enter by the back way. In my enthusiasm I walked past the official entrance. On rounding a bend in the road I espied the big red column, the restored column. It was exactly the right moment, for just as I had reached the bend I was saying to myself—it should be here, this is the spot for it! I feel now that I can set out for any of the sacred places of the earth without guide or compass. Each place has its deity which beckons to you as you approach. In all these spots the earth is unusually quiet— a dynamic passivity, vital as the electric fluids of the cosmos.

It is not only unthinkable, but absolutely impossible, that these sacred spots should one day go the way of modern progress. No machine could survive in this atmosphere. Here the spirit of place rules tyranically, supreme master of past, present and future. What the human spirit achieved in these few nuclei of chaos remains imperishable. Life eddies about these eternal rocks, these silent anchorages in the earth. And often, when examining the relics in the museums, I have had the thought that in rifling the tombs of their relics man is merely abetting the preservation of sanctity. It is well that all the material manifestations should be removed. The museums will perish one day and with them every vestige of man's past achievements. But in the "place" the spirit hovers eternally and willy-nilly man will be drawn back to these centers again and again to rediscover his heritage.

At Knossus particularly, because it is so solidly entrenched, one feels the marvelous therapeutic value of the slow rhythm of life. Everything was done leisurely, one feels. The very features of the race—*what race?*—bespeak this slow, dignified rhythm. The great throne chair of Minos—in itself it speaks volumes. One did not sit down in this seat as one now takes a chair. One lowered the full, majestic body to make a magical contact with the earth. The chair was sunk deep into the bowels of the earth. It was a seat of justice, everything carefully weighed, carefully deliberated. In the legend one thinks of Minos as a monster exacting tribute. When one descends to the seat one feels that he was a great legislator. He was dispensing justice and wisdom. He represented art, peace, industry, joy, well-being. Joy! That is the quality which Knossus breathes even from its sad ruins. And in the faces of the Cretans even to-day there is a light which I have not seen elsewhere in Greece, as yet. The glance is full and bright, without fear and without malice. There is no meanness of soul in the Cretan. He looks out at you from beneath his black turban as the pagans of old must have looked. The sufferings and privations of centuries have not dimmed this bright, honest glance. Aside from the Berbers and the Arabs, or certain tribes in India, the Cretans have the finest human expression I have yet seen. There is not only race and character in the face, but *dignity*, a quality now almost extinct in the human countenance.

Aboard the good ship Frinton, the boat which took me from Athens to Corfu last July—my first trip. Like seeing an old friend. The same crew, same waiters, same maître d'hotel. I am waiting three hours for the boiled rice I ordered when I came aboard—only to find out that they have no rice. Very Greek. Never to say No! Against the pharmacist's orders I order a full dinner. Diarrhoea, or no diarrhoea, I am going to eat. Upstairs in the salon they are playing swing mustic—disques from Athens. My head is full of Nijinsky, the Ballet Russe, Monte Carlo, Vienna, Budapest, London. I have almost forgotten where we are. Crete seems like something in the distant past. I remember, while getting my shoes shined opposite the Fountain Morosini, how good the last glances about were. At the last minute the eye works feverishly, devouring everything like a hungry man. The question always is—will one ever return?

Just as I am about to leave comes an urgent request from Monsieur le Préfet to visit him at his bureau. I go with Alexion and Kafatos, the agricultural expert. It seems the Préfet—Kyrios Stavros Tsoussis—has been looking for me ever since my arrival. He wanted to put his aerodynamic car at my disposal, he wanted me to attend a banquet in my honor, he wanted to let me know how pleased he is to see a stranger from a free country.

Stavros Tsoussis is an extraordinary individual, a figure out of the Renaissance. What he is doing in Candia is beyond me. He has all the makings of an intelligent, capable dictator, a man of action, sharp, decisive, alert, efficient, almost American in his dynamism. It is the first time in my life the police have been searching for me to do me the honors. I tell him so. We talk about Phaestos, about the "peaceful" quality of the Minoan epoch. I leave feeling that I have been in the presence of a man who will be known one day, a man of power. It is the greatest surprise I have had since coming to Greece. Outside his office a ragged little urchin, barefooted, is hanging about. She doesn't seem to be overawed by the presence of the police. In no city of the world have I seen a sight like this. It reminds me of the Académie Pédagogique at Candia. Not finding Alexion I decide to ask permission to inspect the school. I visit one room after another, including the kitchen and the agricultural station in the backyard. How can I describe it? *Human.* Intensely warm and human, as though teacher and pupil were friends, or relatives. In the music class they sing for me—forty or fifty lusty bass voices—Byzantine church music. Then sight-reading from the music book, the strangest music book I have ever seen. All done zestfully, with gusto. They show me the scientific apparatus—for physics and chemistry. They deplore the lack of equipment, talk about the new building. Damn the new building! Keep the old spirit, I say! Greece doesn't need new buildings, new equipment. Greece is doing marvelously with just the bare necessities. Why compete with the rich countries? Why enter a race with overwhelming handicaps? I walk about the crooked streets, peering into the big courtyards. So like Madeira. I am sure of it, though I've never been to Madeira. I stop at a shop to buy some postcards. Some of them are shop-worn. The man leaves me with his wife while he runs home with the cards to clean them (sic!). His wife is French. From Normandy. She talks to me about France. She misses the verdure of Normandy, the cows, the rich pasture lands. She has a sour face, dead eyes, that hateful French way of reducing everything to logic and realism. I begin contradicting her. I was ecstatic about the bare mountains, the dust, the rocks, the blazing sun. She looks at me as if I were crazy. Yes, my dear woman, I like Greece precisely because it *is* Greece and not France. What I like about Greece is its Greekness. Crazy, what? Keep your French garden, your wall around the house, your modest negatives, your subjunctive moods, your logic, your sous. What is good about Greece is that it is illogical, paradoxical, a contradiction from one end to another. But Greece is never "*pale*", never "*gloomy*". Even the artificial eyes in the pharmacist's shop are interesting. Monstrous eyes, for Cyclopean men. . . .

An evening at Kyrios Elliadi's home. During the course of the meal the president of the tailors' association of Candia arrives. "Don't get up," says Elliadi—"it's only my tailor." In a few minutes another visitor, another president of another association. "Where do you come from, gentleman?" he asks me. Follows a thoroughly surrealistic conversation in which we discuss the tailors' art, the war, the expulsion from Asia Minor, the statues along Riverside Drive, N.Y., the Jewish problem, the cost of living for a family of four, the curb market in Wall Street, and so on and so forth.

Elliadi, I must explain, is the British Vice Consul at Candia, an

ertswhile refugee from Smyrna. The evening of my arrival, as I
was sitting alone in the restaurant, he came up to me and asked
if I were Mr. Miller. He wanted me to know that his services were
entirely at my disposal—and, he added, especially because you are
an American! And then he related what I have heard now so often,
the story of the disinterested aid of Americans following upon the
expulsion of the Greeks from Asia Minor. Here was one man who
had vowed never to forget the kindness of the Americans. I was
touched, naturally. I have said many things against my compatriots
at different times, but the fact that they are kind, that they give
without motive other than natural human sympathy is a fact
beyond dispute. Sometimes, in traveling about Greece, in listening
to the tales of Greeks who have worked in the mines in Arizona,
Montana, Alaska, men from the lumber camps, the farms, the
steel mills, the automobile factories, men who ran fruit stands or
restaurants or soda water fountains, florists from Washington
Heights or Cathedral Parkway, sometimes in listening to their
fervid praise of America, I begin to wonder if I am not wrong about
my own country. Another thought often occurs to me, in moments
of loneliness, when the barriers of race and language isolate me
from those about me—the thought that in a vastly diminished
way I am being privileged to experience the emotions of the countless immigrants who have come to America to make a home, to
know some pale reflection of their struggles, their need for com-
radeship, for a wee touch of human sympathy. I try to think what
my life might be if I were obliged to remain in a foreign country,
to earn my living there, to learn the language, to adapt myself to
their ways. The few Americans who have changed their national-
ity have done so under entirely different circumstances than the
immigrant whom we receive. For an American it is a luxury, a
grotesque whim which he is pleased to indulge. It is never an act
of necessity, of despair or desperation. Once an American always
one. Lafcadio Hearn became a true Japanese, but then he was born
of Greek and Irish parents, he was a poet, a dreamer, a visionary.

However, to Mr. Elliadi, Vice Consul from Smyrna—greetings! And thank you for the book you so kindly gave me. I am one American who will never forget Greece or the Greek people. I have a soft spot in my heart for them. Especially for the Greek who interests me above all others—the wretched, forlorn creature without shoes, dressed like a ragamuffin, living by grace of the sun, the nourishing airs, the vitality of the roots of the race. I shudder to think what would become of this vast nameless horde of beggars should the climate ever change. They would die like flies. Nowhere yet have I seen such destitution, nor such manly fortitude. A Frenchman is a continual grumbler, despite the fact that he is the richest man in the world. The poverty-stricken Greek does not grumble. Nor does he dance a jig for his proper tip when he renders you a service. France is the country where perhaps it is true that the sense of justice has been developed to the highest degree. Nevertheless, as Shakespeare long ago pointed out, and long before Shakespeare, Christ, Buddha, Lao Tse, charity comes before justice. And I feel that despite the horrible inequities in Greece, charity, generosity, kindness, sympathy, spontaneity are virtues which the Greeks as a whole possess to a high degree. American charity is of another order—it is unconscious—the gesture of a man whose pockets are full and who cannot be bothered measuring out justice, or counting out sous. But French charity is nil, non-existent. Charity does not fit into the scheme of logic. It is something *"gratuit"*, like André Gide's pseudo-Dostoievskian murders in his cerebral romances. Now then, Mr. Elliadi, I can't say that your book overwhelms me. Though I am unable to believe in your poetic genius I salute you for the friendly gesture you made me at Candia the day I arrived. I am making an imperishable recording of it; it will be for the museum dedicated to human works and in a script forever readable. And a thousand thanks for the boiled rice which you made in order to cure my dysentery. I hope the day will soon be at hand when the town of Candia has a restaurant worthy of its archaeological renown. Good wishes to your tailor friend, President of the Merchant Tailors' Association of Candia. I told you that my grandparents were tailors, but I did not mention that my father was also a tailor and that I myself began as a tailor.

A few hours at Canea . . .

The old town (Canea) most interesting. A real labyrinth. An image of Venice in tatters. But what pleased me the most was a haphazard meeting with a dwarf in the street. A Goya dwarf. It seems there were three monsters on public exhibition in Candia, but I missed them. I contented myself with listening to the music —the Oriental flute. It was a lovely night and the spot well chosen. From the crags above the old hags descended to see what was happening. There was a lot of dust—and mud. The odor of roasted chestnuts and the neighing of little Greek horses. Further on, as I discovered, there was a spectacular site—a great moat surrounding the walls. And there, while listening to the radio with its crazy loudspeakers, I fell into a reverie about the unknown world of Asia. I felt as if I were already in the land of the Hittites. That vast space, emptier than emptiness itself, gave me a nostalgic feeling for prehistoric Asia. The disk with Minoan writing was before my eyes. I saw again the Babylonian tablets I had once been shown at the British Museum. I thought of another style of writing, the most beautiful, the most primitive I had ever seen—the Mayan script. And then of another wondrous one—the Egyptian hieroglyphics which I pondered over for an hour or more one day at the Louvre when in search of the Zodiac of Denderah embedded in the ceiling of the Louvre.

Here a long interruption, thanks to Mr. Machrianos, an engineer who knows every town in Greece. He speaks good English. Why not? He spent his youth in Pittsburgh at the Carnegie Institute. He is a technician, one of the vast army working to reclaim the Greek soil. He knows all about water, malaria, sewage, forests, manure, where there are good hotels, good restaurants. He tells me again of the crazy Greeks who returned from America with money, who open modern hotels in the wildnerness and keep things going in strict American fashion, even if there is not a customer in sight. From the lips of this man I get a bird's eye view of what the government is trying to do—a truly herculean task. His talk confirms my own convictions about Greece. In another twenty years Greece will be unrecognizable. She is adapting herself to the times almost with Japanese alacrity. Islanders are always adaptable. It is the highlander who remains conservative. How will Greece stand when the war is over? Already the politicians envisage the "*appauvrissement*" of the rich countries. Greece is poor. Greece is at the bottom of the ladder. I think of the Japanese again. I see no reason why the Greeks should not emulate them. If ever there should be twenty or thirty million Greeks in the world something fantastic will happen. Their curiosity is unlimited, their energy unbounded. There may be a new Peloponnesian war, with Greece rising to the ascendancy, assuming the hegemony of the Balkans. In any case, the movement is forward. Nothing but an earthquake will stop the headlong rush.

I am forgetting about Canea, the Venetian city. Another maritime people. A mighty people. Canea is far more interesting than Corfu. What a leprous maze of streets, what doors and doorways! In the new part of the city, the Greek section, one feels the airiness of the Greek character The houses straggle towards sea and mountain. There is space between. The light filters in. The children are playing in the sun. A fat woman is standing on a ladder in the middle of the street, trimming a tree. Very Greek. It could be a pioneer town in America, except for the architecture. It is the architecture of nomads who have just settled down to the land. It is not architecture—it is plain refuge, shelter, the body putting a roof over the soul. Inland, towards Phaestos, the construction is still more primitive. We are among the Kalmucks, the Siberians. Everything bequeathed by tradition has been forgotten. Like the Pueblo Indians of New Mexico the Greeks have dug themselves into the rock. The trog-

lodyte's instinct prevails. One is in the land of hurricanes, torna-
does, cloudbursts, sand storms, heat waves, glaciers, avalanches,
pests, ghosts, demons, what not. Man digs in.

I am reading the life of Nijinsky, the man whose life itself was a
great piece of art. He is standing on the deck of the ocean liner,
enraptured by the first sight of the skyscrapers. He begins to leap
in the air like a kangaroo. He wants to ride up and down the ele-
vators all day. He likes the American bathrooms, the express trains
riding through the city in the air. He sees that there is opportunity
here for every one. He is lionized. He buys a car. He runs the car
backwards downhill to test the brakes. He is intoxicated. A year
later he confesses—"America is not a country in which to create.
One must have peace and quiet." Five years later he is in the mad-
house. Peace and quiet forever now. He is at rest. He has left the
earth. As in the Spectre de la Rose, he made one mighty leap out of
the window and into space. He is hanging there now—in space—a
victim of the times. Do the Greeks know the mad diary Nijinsky
left behind? What will they say of it? It is important to know about
Nijinsky. He tried to do what Milarepa, the great Tibetan poet and
sage did. But he was not strong enough. He was too much of an
artist. There was not enough evil in him . . .

Nijinsky's final obsession was with the circle. Curious for a man
whose particular form of insanity is described as "schizophrenia".
Nijinsky's whole struggle in life was to become a complete individual. By nature he was dual. The transformation from a homo-
sexual to a happily married man was in itself a great triumph.
Nijinsky wanted more than that. He wanted a union with God.
Finally he identified himself with God, and was pronounced insane. Up to the last he was kind, gentle, tolerant, forgiving. He
strove to get beyond the sphere of art; he was perhaps the supreme
artist of our time—"*le dieu de la danse*," as he was called. His
error consisted, not in seeking God, but in forsaking art. Godhood
is not attained through piety, but through art. Art is the whole
from which we cannot escape. Art makes the circle, because it

" Silence! This is my marriage with God!"
Nijinsky

" Now I will dance you the war, with
its suffering, with its destruction, with its
death. The war which you did not prevent and so you are also responsible for."
Nijinsky.

" We do not become insane — we
are born it." (Prof. Bleuler)

" Let him dream his dreams!"
(Professors Freud, Jung, Kreplin, Bleuler, et alia)

"Mr. Nijinsky is the sanest person in
the whole of St. Moritz Dorf."
(the nurse)

" I want to talk to somebody,
who would understand me....."
Nijinsky

_____

Maintenant il parle avec Dieu.
Enfin il y avait quelqu'un
qui l'a compris
Hau.

embraces all, God included. Nijinsky was confused. He forgot his own true words—"there are no bad people, only stupid ones." He thought religion was beyond art, but it is not. Art includes religion. Art is man, on his way to ordination. There is no beyond—there is *it*, the nameless, which is eternal. Wholeness is achieved not by overcoming duality, but by embracing it. Only in spirit are we one. In life we are myriad. Insanity is part of life. It is one of the manifestations of wholeness. Insanity is one of many ways to salvation. The tragedy is merely that the insane are unaware of their bliss. They *are* bliss. In the *Possessed* Kirillov kills himself because he has discovered the secret of happiness. To discover God before one's time is a form of insanity. The Greeks too committed suicide when they arrived at their plenum. God himself commits suicide over and over, in order to realize himself anew.

I put down these reflections upon finishing the story of Nijinsky's life. It is a life which touches me to the core. They say he is constantly daydreaming, but that he has not lost his memory. *"He knows that he is Nijinsky."* I find these words singularly expressive—startling, in fact. We are living in a period which constantly threatens to annihilate not only our personality but our very identity. The extreme prevalence of schizophrenia (now admittedly the disease claiming the greatest number of victims—in America, at least) is but the reflection of the times. We shall not make a new world until we make new men. To the vast majority the thought is terrifying. It means death in the most potent form—death to the present order of men. . . .

Eleusis. My friend Ghika showing me about the ruins in the dark, striking matches to point out the mysterious symbols cut into the stones. To find Greece dark at six in the evening is one of those phenomena which, despite all evidence, it is difficult to believe. "In Greece there is never night," said a Frenchman, "only the absence of day." This may be true of Greece in the abstract, but it is not true of such places as Mycenae or Eleusis. On the contrary, there is at Eleusis a darkness far more profound than that which the night brings. Eleusis is shrouded in a pall, as though while still in the womb one's mother should go in mourning. The very site, it seems to me, was chosen for its blackness. We came upon the village as the sun was setting. We rushed upon it in a swift, noiseless Packard. Never was a sky more filled with color than this one. The light was extinguished in a blaze of flaming banners. And then suddenly blackness, total annihilation of light. A death, to be followed by a resurrection. After the most extraordinary sunset greens, the whole sky like a sinking lake of moss, suddenly the only tone discernible is the rusty brown of the worn steps, a hoary monk's brown, a mysterious waxen patina which excites the retina. The ruins sink back, not into the night, but into time, into the slippery well of the past from which each day the light vainly strives to rescue them. Even the archaeologist—indefatigable beast of burden that he is, mole, worm, jackass, pedant, slave—even this monster seems here to admit his defeat. The mystery refuses to yield to the spade and the chemical retort. Men will have to develop other means, other organs of apprehension and discernment. Eleusis is grand in its obscurity. A *soft* grandeur, a warm, inspiring intimacy, a human, all-too-human immediacy. It is the very antithesis of the Hindu or the Tibetan mystery. It was in shrinking to his natural human proportions that man here created the Greek attitude towards the mystery. Here one perceives that the temple of the spirit is a man-made habitation.

And this was my very first impression of Athens when I came upon it for the first time last July. The first things which struck me were the little churches of Byzantine cast. One especially, which is sunk into the ground, which is exactly the right size for human worship. Even the new public buildings on University Street appealed to me, for the same reason. Similarly at the Acropolis—the little temples—gems. Whereas the Parthenon leaves me cold.

It is stupid to say so, but I prefer the Theseion. I like its squatness. I feel at home there. The Parthenon shuts one out, perhaps even more by its perfection than by its size. I like it best from a great distance—from Eden, for instance—that first glimpse one gets as one turns the road. From this distance it is a gem. The building which most excites me, of course, is Agamemnon's tomb. Here there is an element which is lacking in the Parthenon—mystery. For me this tomb ranks as the most awesome, the most thrilling construction by man's hand. I felt when I entered that most esoteric portal that I was in the presence of magical spirits. Other heroes out of the past may be dead. Agamemnon—for me—is still alive. If you stand there quietly and reverently you will hear his voice. He was not a demi-god, as the books tell us—he was a god, full-blown, and he lives on, even in death, a more powerful spirit than all the conquerors of the earth combined. The body should never have been removed. Anyway, it was only the corporeal body that was removed. If you stand in a certain place in the tomb and pronounce his name softly he will answer you. (Katsimbalis is a witness to the fact.) The immortal body of Agamemnon is still there, in the crypt which to this day smells of death. This crypt is still permeated with the odor of his body. Nothing can eliminate it. What I am trying to say, and I repeat it over and over, is that between this age of gold and the Periclean one there is an incalculable void. In the span of a dozen centuries or so the corpus of magic was shattered. The Africans are closer in spirit to Agamemnon's epoch than the civilized members of society. With the African the soul is exteriorized—it has not yet found its resting place, its dwelling, in the human temple. Agamemnon, I feel,

— — — — — —

"*Cosmos*". Katsimbalis asks what do I mean by cosmos! I mean the world, of course, as does any Greek when he pronounces the word. Only with this difference—that when originally the Greek said cosmos it meant "*the* world"—not *a* world, or world. To-day "world" means anything and everything. There is no world any-

more. There are only worlds—plural always. *The* world—"cosmos"
—is gone. To make a world again, a cosmos, we must have new
men with new eyes. Man must be re-endowed with a soul. This
world, *our* world of to-day, belongs not to man, nor even to the
beast, but to the machine. *Alors*, down with the world! Up with
the Cosmos.

— —   — — — —

embodied his own soul. This gesture of embrace was the ultimate
link between man and the cosmos. It definitely centered the
human being, gave him his cosmic stance, cosmic proportions.
Since that time the center has been shifted. We are functioning
along an axis which is only obliquely polarized. Nothing more
vividly illustrates the contrast between then and now than the
present war. It is the difference between body warfare and abstract
warfare. In the shock of mortal embrace of old there was a marriage
with death which was fructifying. The deaths to-day are merely
statistical. Witness everywhere the tomb to the Unknown Soldier.
Our heroes are anonymous. There is no one whose memory we can
reverence, no spirit to salute. We stand with bowed heads before
the scattered remnants of a body, the body of a man whose identity
has been lost. "We who are fast losing our identity salute you, O
nameless one!" We are fighting in the air, like great carrion birds.
We destroy whole populations by pressing a button. The enemy is
everywhere, animate and inanimate. Everything inspires fear,
dread, panic. We are fighting our own shadows—a guerilla war
with ghosts. Such is civilization. Such is the Steel Age, outwardly
so concrete, innerly utterly abstract. The mightiest constructions
are shattered like bubbles. A breath can blow down a fortress. The
hand of a child can wipe out centuries of effort. Idiocy. Sheer
idiocy.

Betty Ryan is a young American woman who seduced me with her faithful, ravishing descriptions of Greece. I spent hours, whole days even, listening to her. The miracle is that all she told me was true. Everywhere I go in Greece I discover the imprints she left in traveling from one end of the country to the other, and never attracting the slightest attention. I am familiar wih the works of those who have written about the marvels of Greece, but by comparison with the words of this unknown young woman their words seem pale. I feel obliged to extend her my homage here and now, homage to a pure, precise vision. God bless her for the privilege she granted me in listening to her sweet, ecstatic voice.
Lying in bed amidst the ruins of Athens. Suddenly, in my feverish state, there comes to my mind the very distinct pre-image of Athens which I formed as a result of listening to Betty Ryan. Suddenly I am no longer in the Athens I know but in the Athens I created at the Villa Seurat, Paris. This Athens is more open, offering a view of sea and mountain at once. It is a four in the afternoon Athens with no trams, no auto trucks, no shrieking noises. There are modern buildings but they are in the background. This Athens, strangely enough, I have seen a number of times on my way to and from Corfu. At Zante I saw it in the abstract. Zante is for me a dream place. Every Greek port has this insistent white dream plastic. Every tiny port gives the illusion of a new world in genesis, of a nucleus which will spread like a web. Zante, however, obsesses me. Perhaps because of the deserted quay with the single palm tree. Perhaps because I first glimpsed it through a port-hole at the very moment I was writing about it and not knowing that it was Zante. Perhaps because I had discovered it in a dream which fused with reality. I wanted to come to the frontier of a new world, a very tiny world which would answer to every demand. Zante seems like such a world. For me it is the threshold of Greece. And here I would install as the first queen of the dynasty, the dazzling Niki

Rhally. Every Greek island should be ruled over by a queen. They belong essentially to the women of Greece. Somehow, the more I see of Greece the more I believe that the women were always predominant, always the unseen power. Often the man seems a mere appendage. When you roam the countryside it is the female figure which dominates the landscape. The woman is active and sustaining. She carries a double burden always.

I am all for the Greek women! For their total emancipation. The dowry must be abolished. One must stop trading in virginity! It is a disgrace to Greece. Every Greek woman is worth her salt. To expect her to furnish a dowry in addition to her assets—of pack-bearing mule, draught-horse, water-carrier, ditch-digger, day laborer, wet-nurse, child-bearer, comforter, concubine, cook and general roustabout—is a little too much. The Greek woman should become the celestial bee of the hive. The spindle-shanked drones of the pseudo-aristocracy who sit eating sweets dressed in furs in mid-September should be dethroned. The Greek woman whom I respect and would pay honor to is the one who is walking in the mud in bare feet with a pack on her back and an ache in her womb. This is the woman I would train to walk upright, to grow five toes and not six. I have passed through villages where almost the entire male population was sitting outdoors moping in the sun. This is not a proof of male ascendancy, or superiority—it is a sign of degeneration. And these are the duffers who expect their women to come to them pure, or at any rate, *technically* pure, i.e. virgins. Bad 'cess to them! May they die of the pox, all of them! In all my travels I have never seen such beautiful women as in Greece. Nor have I ever seen women so miserably treated. And though it may sound crazy to say so, I have a feeling that that is why the Greek cat is such a miserable specimen. The cat seems to have incarnated the mute hunger and misery and dejection of the women. It is not properly a cat at all—it is a sort of furtive scavenger. The lowest of them all is the Corfiote variety, with a loathesome, repulsive snout or muzzle such as distinguishes the eater of carrion. Neither is the Greek dog much to boast of. He is either too submissive, slinking, scab-eaten or else vicious and rapacious. A bad sign! But in both cases it is the man who is responsible. . .

The one creature I had never expected to meet in Greece, and one that seems to be especially favored, is the turkey. The turkey seems to bob up everywhere and is treated like a pet. A pet to be eaten one day. Which is very Greek again. For in Greece it is the drama of voraciousness which is supreme. The incest theme is a polite expression of the need to devour what is nearest and dearest. There is a kind of ingratitude among the Greeks which the foreigner is quick to smell out. It is the evil flower, one might say, of anarchy. Ultimately the Greek stands alone. Ultimately he devours his own progeny. It is in the blood. I sometimes think the Greek is older than any of the known races of the world. I find him at times curiously like the Australian aborigine. The way he laughs, for example, when he is caught cheating. He does everything with a bald face. A part of him—the social part—has not developed at all. That is why, perhaps, the cafés are so lamentably sterile and lugubrious. That is why he falls for American gadgets while understanding nothing of their raison d'être. Towards mechanical things he behaves like a Chinaman. He can adapt himself to any device or invention, but the spirit of it is quite beyond him. If one could Americanize the country overnight it would become a huge heap of scrap-iron in a few years. The Minoan man was not a Greek. He was an invader who probably dispersed or enslaved the autocthonous race. He was the survivor of an old and unknown race. He did not evolve on Cretan soil. He was already formed, developed and running to seed when he landed there. That is my belief. I am not a scholar and it is quite likely I am wrong, but that is my opinion just the same. Where the Greek springs from is a mystery to me. I don't take any stock in the theories of the ethnological savants. I say the Greek is also very old—but culturally young. The primitive quality in him far outweighs the cultural. One has only to see those pre-classical Picassos in the

Ethnological Museum at Athens to understand the distinction. Those island statues without name or origin speak far more eloquently than the ruins of the Acropolis. The best things of Greece are still hidden away in the earth, I am sure of it. In the age to come, when man begins to exhume the marvels hidden beneath the seas, we shall perhaps discover the true origins of Greece. . .

All this is very unorthodox and perhaps very American. But it is also a testimonial of my reverence for the true Greek spirit. I cannot accept the dates and the explanations of the scholars. I prefer to make my own history of Greece, a history which will correspond with the incomprehensible marvels I have witnessed with my own eyes. When I go to Delphi I shall consult my own oracles. I shall put my ear to the ground, like a good American Indian, and listen. I shall say a prayer there for the Greece which is to come, which I see everywhere in bud and which promises a splendid harvest. I shall make a hymn to the light, the light of Attica. I shall put in an extra plea of grace and forgiveness for the women of Smyrna, for their off-spring down to the 42nd generation. I shall ask that Agamemnon be restored to power and glory and that Phaestos shall be reinhabited by a new race of queens. I shall request that the mountains be kept bare and the diet lean. I shall not ask that riches be heaped upon you but that the spirit which animates the sacred places be kept alive. Greece belongs not to the legislators but to the gods. Let the gods walk the earth again, say I!

Addenda:

And now, my dear Seferiades, how am I ever to make you understand how deeply grateful I am for the bounteous hospitality you
showered me with? Will I one day be able to show you America—
the Golden Gate, the Grand Canyon, the petrified forest of Arizona,
the slaughter-house in Chicago, the skyscrapers, the famous Zieg-
feld beauties, the parks I sleep in, the comfort stations, the ferry-
boats, etc. etc.? Who knows? I almost hope not. I prefer to come
back here again, quickly, and visit with you and Katsimbalis and
Ghika and Antonio and Tsatsos all the places we did not have time
to see. I would like to find an unknown island in the Aegean and
set you up as an emperor, a Byzantine emperor. I would like to see
you blossom there in a soft Smyrna way, see you dance among
your megalithian poems, your Mycenean rhythms. I should like
to come upon you in old age, a poet saturated with his own wines,
giving off the fragrant resin of his own verse.

Yours for the Resurrection!

Henry Miller

THE
WATERS REGLITTERIZED

THE SUBJECT OF WATER COLOR
IN SOME OF ITS MORE LIQUID PHASES.

by Henry Miller

From Henry to Emil
in moments of inspiration or
perplexity, with gratitude for
having put me on the right Path.

Begun in bed this
22nd of February, 1939—anniversary
of George Washington's birth.
(The Battle of the Wilderness)

1973

PREFACE

T HIS LITTLE VOLUME, originally written by hand in a printer's dummy, was intended exclusively for my friend Emil Schnellock. It was my pleasure to write several little books in this manner, for my intimate friends, during the last few years of my stay in Paris. The last one, written for the poet George Seferis, of Greece, I wrote on the island of Hydra. Because they were written with the pen, and not on the typewriter, they all have a direct, intimate quality. They were done in my spare time, usually in the course of a few weeks.

This one is particularly dear to me because it deals with "the water color mania." After about twenty years of struggle with the medium I am about to be given an exhibition in Paris. It is an odd coincidence, and a most gratifying one for me, that this exhibition, which I regard as an important one, should be held in Paris where, after twenty years of struggle with another medium, I at last succeeded in getting my first book (*Tropic of Cancer*) published.

To be sure, I have had a number of shows in America. None of them, however, except the one in Hollywood, which was sponsored by Clara Grossman, has meant much to me. (Nor did they mean much to the public, I suspect.)

I must immediately add that from American painters I had much, much encouragement. Two men in particular I must mention in this connection—Abraham Rattner and Bezalel Schatz. For a month or two, while living in New York, I had the privilege of working beside Rattner in his studio. It was an unforgettable experience. I have spoken of it at some length in *Remember to Remember*, where I tried to give a full length portrait of this great American artist. As for "Lilik" Schatz and what he has done, not only for me but for all his intimate friends, I will say just this—he is the spiritual son and heir of Max Jacob.

But to come back to this little document . . . My primary reason for permitting it to become public now is to pay a debt of gratitude to my old friend and comforter, Emil Schnellock. It was he who inspired me to continue after I had made a start. (I needed plenty of encouragement because in school I had always been given up as hopeless, that is, in the art class.) During my ten years in Paris we maintained a steady and voluminous correspondence. On my return to America in 1940, I visited my friend Emil in Virginia. One day he brought out a huge trunk crammed with the letters, manuscripts, notes, photos, plans, projects and documents of all sorts which I had sent him over the years. It was a staggering collection and testified more eloquently to our friendship than anything I may say here.

The other day I had a letter from Joan Miro, and the following day one from Marc Chagall. I read aloud to my wife. When I looked up she had tears in her eyes. "How simply and beautifully they write!" she remarked. "And they are such great men!" Yes, that is the way of the European, the man of genius. He goes to the core immediately. A post-card from one of these birds says more and means more than a long essay from one of our pundits.

A few days later I pick up a little book sent me by André Breton (*La Lampe dans l'Horloge*) and I find him quoting from a letter I wrote him a year or so ago. It was not an extraordinary letter, and certainly not a literary one. But Breton thought enough of it to single it out for attention. This almost never happens to me with American writers. In fact, I hardly ever hear from an American writer of any prominence.

Why do I speak of this? To point out another glaring aspect of the situation in which American artists find themselves. No communion. No real intercommunication. No concern for the vital, subtle things which mean everything to a writer, painter or musician. We live in a void spanned by the most intricate and elaborate means of communication. Each one occupies a planet to himself. But the messages never get through!

In the same vein. . . . My friend Schatz of Palestine hands me a little book the other day. "Read it," he says, "I think you'll get a kick out of it." As soon as he's gone I glance at it. It's by Antonin Artaud, the French poet who died a short while ago. The book was written in 1947, after Artaud's release from the asylum where he had spent nine years.

I was so tired I had no desire to begin a book, however small, before going to bed. But I happened to turn a few pages and I was caught. Holding the book under the dying lamp, I read like a madman. I could scarcely believe my eyes. With his last breath, you might say, Artaud writes about that other madman, Van Gogh. Incredible language. The language which only a man of genius can summon to pay homage to another man of genius. Not merely exalted, but mad. (Mad like de Nerval, like Swift, like Nijinsky.) Corrective madness. Tinged with the vitriol of scorn, hatred, contempt and disdain for the "sane," for the bourgeois spirits, for the aesthetes, the patrons and the patronizers of art. Ditto for the whole breed of psychiatric quacks into whose hands men like Van Gogh and Artaud inevitably fall.

I could go on like this indefinitely. This is how we rambled on when we met, my friend Emil and I. I'm thinking of the period between the first two world wars. Then I knew no French, alas! I read only those authors, those books, which our publishers charily selected for us to read in translation. In 1940, when we met again, I was like a man who had been through the fires of redemption.

For ten years I had been steeped in amazing experiences—physical, moral, spiritual. Many of these I had confided to Emil in my letters. Some I deliberately withheld until the day we would meet again. "My friend," I used to say to myself, "just wait till I get back there! The things I have to relate will drive you mad." Today, almost ten years later, I am still telling him about those wonderful days when I lived in Paris.

Albert Cossery lives in the 18th arrondissement. He has just had his third book published—*Les Fainéants dans la vallée fertile.* James Laughlin, of New Directions, says he will probably bring it out in translation. I hope so. Only a handful of Americans seem to have read the first book— *Men God Forgot.* In his second book (*The House of Certain Death*), which New Directions will bring out shortly, Cossery has taken for his theme a crack in the wall. It is a symbolic crack, *bien entendu,* the sort of crack which split the world egg in two in mythologic times. Cossery is desperately poor and therefore not so gay, but growing richer day by day. A fourth book is now germinating, but he will not begin it unless he is assured at least a million francs in advance. He is an Egyptian, I ought to add. Perhaps the most unusual one the world has seen for centuries.

Before I go too far astray I must say a word about Utrillo. Some people will undoubtedly misinterpret my words of applause for the pork dealer's remark. I should not want it to be thought that *I* regard Utrillo's work as "sordid." No sir! Utrillo is one of the figures in contemporary painting who is almost Christ-like. And that is why I mentioned Francis Carco's glowing portrait of him. To my knowledge this book by Carco has never been translated into English. Why? Are there not thousands of people in America who admire Utrillo's work? Is his life not a legendary one?

Carco himself, incidentally, is a man to whom attention ought to be given.

I have just returned from my usual morning hike in the forest. Every time I enter this forest three names come to my lips: Hamsun, Débussy and Derain. (I never think of Thoreau, oddly enough.) Knut Hamsun I think of because of *Pan, Victoria, A Wanderer Plays on Muted Strings*. Débussy because of *Pelléas et Mélisande*. Derain because of certain landscapes in which the earth is all gold. The entrance to the forest is like a décor on which these three Europeans collaborated. Golden music, mysterious murmurings ("like a million nothings," as Hamsun says), nostalgic reveries. All contained in the hollow of a little dell strewn with the rotting trunks of dead redwoods.

When I penetrate a little farther, when I find myself following the banks of the little stream, I inevitably begin communing with Jean Giono. Every once in a while I get a letter from this *Jean le bleu*, usually followed by another new book of his. Every book Giono writes is a paean and invocation. Perhaps that is why they do not sell in America. The underlying theme is the same—*Que Ma Joie Demeure!*

I open the window of my little studio to make water. The poppies are in full bloom. Which reminds me of Van Gogh and the little book by Antonin Artaud: Van Gogh, *le suicidé de la société*. (K. Editeur, 2, rue des Beaux-Arts, Paris.)

I quote a few passages at random . . .

"Qui ne sent pas la bombe cuite et le vertige comprimé n'est pas digne d'être vivant. C'est le dictame que le pauvre Van Gogh en coupe de flamme se fit un devoir de manifester."

"En face d'une humanité de singes lâches et de chiens

mouillés, la peinture de Van Gogh aura été celle d'un temps où il n'eut pas d'âme, pas d'esprit, pas de conscience, pas de pensée, rien que des éléments premiers tour à tour enchainés et déchainés."

"C'est ainsi que Van Gogh est mort suicidé, parce que c'est le concert de la conscience entière qui n'a pu plus le supporter."

"Et il avait raison Van Gogh, on peut vivre pour l'infinie, ne se satisfaire que d'infinie, il y a assez d'infinie sur la terre et dans les sphères pour rassasier mille grands génies, et si Van Gogh n'a pas pu combler son désir d'en irradier sa vie entière, c'est que la société le lui a interdit. Carrément et consciemment interdit. Il y a eu un jour les éxécuteurs de Van Gogh, comme il y a eu ceux de Gérard de Nerval, de Baudelaire, d'Edgar Poe, et de Lautréamont. Ceux qui un jour lui ont dit: Et maintenant, assez, Van Gogh, à la tombe, nous en avons assez de ton génie, quant à l'infinie, c'est pour nous l'infinie."

Next we shall speak of coloring a dead man—that is to say, his face, his body, or any naked part that may be visible either on a panel or a wall ... You must use no rosy tints, because dead persons have no color ... As I showed you how to paint several kinds of beards on walls, in the same way paint on panels, and so paint the bones of Christians or rational creatures with this same flesh color.

And here ends this unseemly preface to the little book on the more liquid phases of the aquarelle which was written expressly for my old and steadfast friend Emil in the reverence of God and of the Virgin Mary, and of St. Francis and of John the Baptist and generally of all the saints, big, little or mediocre, and in the reverence of

Cimabue, of Uccello, of Piero della Francesca, of Hieronymus Bosch, of Breughel the Elder, of Van Gogh, Utrillo, Picabia, Rouault and Rattner, for the pleasure, the edification and the liberation of all who would dabble in the medium.

Henry "Cennini" Miller
March 31st, 1949   *Big Sur, California*

LET US NOW BURNISH GOLD, FOR THE TIME IS COME THAT WE SHOULD DO SO.

The
Waters Reglitterized

IN THIS ROOM where I lie I am surrounded with paintings—Nancy's wild Ionian horses, Reichel's ethnological study of wigwams, which is a masterpiece in its genre, his Rosicrucian abstract on glass, the "failed" tapestry which I rescued from the waste basket, the girl in the red hat which is the cover design for the child's book I gave you—and several of my own recent attempts. One of these, in which I used some Chinese white, is an astounding advance on my other "self portraits." I say self-portraits, because, as Anaïs aptly remarked one day, it is always the same face, whether it be a Chinese sage, an African Negro, a war victim or a madman. This one has the real color of flesh in the face, of which I am rather proud. For me, to acquire the slightest technique is always a long but joyous process. My water colors are always voyages of adventure and, whether "successful" or unsuccessful, they give me real satisfaction. I can swim in their presence just as gratefully as if they were Picassos or

Rembrandts. I am never totally disappointed in them, no matter how bad the attempt.

But all this is preliminary to the thought I had in mind when I began. That was a sudden recollection of the night I stood with Joe O'Reagan in front of a department store window—on Livingston Street, Brooklyn, I believe—and took in with all my senses the Turners hanging there. Of course I had begun before, if I remember rightly. I had begun with a box of child's paints and a very bad brush, and a piece of wrapping paper from the butcher shop. I did a copy of George Grosz's self-portrait as *Number One*. That, I vividly remember because of the delight I had in discovering that I could really do something which faintly resembled the original. (Later I had a similar shock, when I did likenesses of my mother and sister from life—in black and white. They thought me a little cracked at the time to be so earnest about such a matter, especially when I was without a job and penniless.)

Everything, however, dates back to your studio on 50th Street, where I got the original impulse, watching you at work and listening to your very sage explanations of the reason for this and that. I remember another period, when I was installed with June at Remsen Street, reading Walter Pater's *Renaissance* and pumping you about not only Botticelli but the Italian Primitives. I can almost hear you again as you discoursed most eloquently on Cimabue and Giotto. And then one day it was Uccello!

Well, during my visit to London recently I saw a Uccello at the National Gallery. You probably know which one I mean—a battle scene, with a marvelous rising background. I studied it for a long while, feeling finally that it was as much of a mystery as ever. (Anything I profoundly like, I notice, always remains a *mystery* to me! It is as true of writing as of music or painting. For example, in literature, no matter how much I know and recognize of "technique," books like Hamsun's *Mysteries*, Dostoievski's *Eternal Husband* and Nijinsky's *Diary* will always be *MYSTERY*. And if you will not think me vain to say so, now and then, in rereading passages of my own work, I feel the same thing. It makes me feel grand—and awed and subdued, at the same time.)

But to come back to that Uccello in the National Gallery—it was only this time that I suddenly realized how *modern* the picture is. How modern Uccello is! Cézanne is an intellectual boy by comparison. And Van Gogh! Why Van Gogh is just a tortured neurasthenic! Uccello taught me a great deal. And how, I ask myself, could his followers have failed to learn? How could we have had such terrible gaps in the real tradition of painting? What monstrosities of learning and bad taste lie between him and Picasso, let us say. Uccello revealed a grandeur and simplicity of soul. He was eloquent in *deed*, not in mere conception or technique. He went straight from vision to the canvas. He did not merely depict a battle-scene. He depicted the state of his, Uccello's, soul at the moment. The canvas is full of soul, full of noble *feeling*. With this soul feeling one can paint or dance or sing or build pyramids. Feeling, feeling. Van Gogh asserts it in a *maladif* way. But Uccello is healthy feeling, strong, contained emotion, a balanced universe—the equilibrium established from within, from his relationship with God, and not from a knowledge of the Golden Rule.

I have noticed, to speak of little things, the great difference in results, when sitting down calmly and undisturbed to do a water color, as against those feverish rushes in between times, when the idea of "doing something" seems paramount.

The remarkable thing to observe, in children's work (as you will see from the book I sent) is that the child gives the impression of having done it with his whole being. They

surrender themselves completely to what is in hand.
Whereas even the biggest artist has to wage a constant
fight against distraction. He is conscious not only of the
future opinions of the critics, the price it will fetch (or *not*
fetch!), the value of his tubes, the nicety of his choice of
color or line, but also the temperature of the room, the
stains on the floor, the bath he forgot to take, and so on.

For one like myself, who is not *obliged* to do water
colors for a living, how wonderful that feeling, as happens
sometimes, when coming home about midnight, the place
extremely quiet, the light giving just the right glow about
my work table, my senses keenly alive, yet not so sharp as
to push me on to further writing, (a sort of sifting-of-the-
ashes feeling, the fire warm but dying), I sit down before
the little pad, determined to do just *one* water color in
peace and harmony. To paint in this way is like communing with oneself—and with all the world too. I seem to
carry on a perpetual conversation. The colors talk to me. I
cajole them, I implore them. And, in the right mood, I will
take infinite pains, for some unknown reason, to mix a
little splotch of color which will fill about an eighth of an
inch on the paper.

But one of the moments I like best, after having done
what I imagine to be my utmost, is the realization that it
won't do at all. I decide to convert the quiet, static picture
in front of me into a live, careless, free and easy thing. I
strike out boldly with whatever comes to hand—pencil,
crayon, brush, charcoal, ink—anything which will de-
molish the studied effect obtained and give me fresh
ground for experiment. I used to think that the striking
results obtained in this fashion were due to accident, but I
no longer am of this mind. Not only do I know today that it
is the method employed by some very famous painters
(Rouault immediately comes to mind), but, I recognize
that it is often the same method which I employ in

writing. I don't go *over* my canvas, in writing, like the meticulous Fraenkel does with his drafts, but I keep breaking new ground until I reach the level of exact expression, leaving all the trials and gropings there, but raising them in a sort of spiral circumnavigation, until they make a solid under-body or under-pinning, whichever the case may be. And this, I notice, is precisely the ritual of life which is practiced by the man who evolves. He doesn't go back, figuratively, to correct his errors and defects: he transposes and converts them into virtues. He makes wings of his larval cerements.

That last "self-portrait" on the wall, which has the appearance of a medieval alchemist, contains a discovery connected with "ears" which pleases me no end. Ears are a bugaboo for me—just as fingers and necks. I had used up all my knowledge of ears—and still they looked like cauliflowers or kohlrabies. Gradually, in working in towards the face from the outside, with more and more transparency, more and more magic, I finally eliminated the ears altogether. And then, as by a stroke of genius (sic!), I slashed a few stigmata on the cheeks, thus giving myself the unconsciously desired aspect of one who had endured many trials, who had perhaps sacrificed his ears for a higher purpose, but who was none the less "all there" *avec ou sans oreilles.* The judicious use of a little Chinese white heightens the mystery and gives luminosity to the intent regard of the visionary who perhaps in a dream had seen the philosopher's stone.

If one day this particular effort should be displayed in the window of the Gotham Book Mart, where I am sending it shortly, it would give me intense pleasure to have you stop and examine it. Still greater pleasure, I might add, if you would go inside and inquire who did it. And the most extreme pleasure, need I say, if after inquiring the price of this masterpiece, you would say, "Wrap it up, please, I'll take it with me." To make sure you will recognize it (!) I shall inscribe on the back of it "*The Philosopher's Stone, in memory of my friend Emil Schnellock who initiated me into the mysteries of Chinese white.*" You will find the stone just at the base of the neck. It is a little patch of under-painting which I left untouched. For *you* Emil, at $1.98.

And now, as I am filled with chills and fever, I will lay the pen aside and dream of the Uccellos we used to talk about—I then in the height of ignorance and you patient and instructive . . .

An additional thought while eating lunch at my work-table and looking at my water color through the reflection in the mirror. For the first time in my experience I suddenly see that the bluish white rays I ran down the man's chest are really vaporous streaks of luminosity and not just paths of a blue color mixed with a little white. When I am in the Metro, waiting for a train, I instinctively study the posters—and that has to do with tricks of shadow, flashes of stuff, differentiation of texture through line, color or shape. I never get anywhere because I simply cannot hold the remembrance of the technique I have studied and the efficacy of which I perceive. I see only what the artist intended me to perceive—that is, a crease in the trousers, not a thin black line with an edge of parallel white. In my own work I only see the "causes"—never the effects. Only now and then, when a visitor comes and begins telling me what he sees in the painting, do I begin to see these things myself. I see only my efforts and abortions—never the desired result. I remember once Reichel coming and criticizing a water color I had just finished, and which I was rather unusually proud of because I thought I had been more than usually successful.

It was a memory picture of the Parc Montsouris—the lake with the swans, etc. Reichel said, "I don't like so much childish paintings." Implying that I had *tried* to paint like a child! I was flattered as well as dumbfounded. But I wasn't at all trying to imitate a child. I was doing my utmost. That he had made a distinction between this picture and others I had shown him baffled me. Where was his sense of criticism? Couldn't he see that they were all fundamentally "childish?" Another time, looking at a hasty, freakish portrait of Fred which I had just finished, he remarked—"What a cruel conception of an *ami*!" But I hadn't the slightest tinge of cruelty in me when doing it. If I had given Fred an idiotic expression it was because the brush had failed me. I was looking at him intently, while doing it, and the result was what apparently horrified Reichel. He was crediting me with a power and control which I have never possessed.

Now, in writing, if someone had made that remark about a piece of portraiture, I would have accepted it silently as a just criticism, even if, as sometimes happens, I had had no malice in the fore-front of my brain. But in writing, you see, I know I am responsible. I know every trick—where to use a semi-colon instead of a dash, when to give a short stabbing thrust, and when to wax loquacious or even circumlocuitous—*even when to stammer!* But I know, too, that beyond a certain point I am no longer responsible. At a certain point the man in me gets the better of the artist. The artist does, can, and will lie—for effect. But not the man! In the realm of water color I am neither of these two creatures: I am simply the blind instrument of chance. I work according to the "Principle of Least Action." What I do not know counts more than what I do know. I should not really sign my name to these things—I am an anonymous creature, a neophyte, a stutterer and stammerer in form and color. You follow me?

The greatest joy, and the greatest triumph, in art, comes at the moment when, realizing to the fullest your grip over the medium, you deliberately sacrifice it in the hope of discovering a vital hidden truth within you. It comes like a reward for patience—this freedom of mastery which is born of the hardest discipline. *Then,* no matter what you do or say, you are absolutely right and nobody dare criticize you. I sense this very often in looking at Picasso's work. The great freedom and spontaneity he reveals is born, one feels, because of the impact, the pressure, the support of the whole being which, for an endless period, has been subservient to the discipline of the spirit. The most careless gesture is as right, as true, as valid, as the most carefully planned strokes. *This I know,* and nobody could convince me to the contrary. Picasso here is only demonstrating a wisdom of life which the sage practices on another, higher level.

This morning, awake at five o'clock, the room almost dark still, I lay awake quietly meditating about the essay I would get up to write, and at the same time, as though playing a duet, watching the gradual change of colors in my paintings beside the bed, as the light slowly increased. I had the strange sensation then of imagining what might happen to those colors should the light continue to increase in strength *beyond full daylight.* And from thinking about the unknown color gamut to the forms themselves and then to their significance—what a world of conjecture I explored! In that moment I was able, so to speak, to place myself in a future which may one day be realized. I saw not only what I might one day be able to do, but also I saw this—that the anticipation of the event was an augury of the deed itself. Suddenly I realized how it had been with the struggle to express myself in writing. I saw back to the period when I had the most intense, exalted visions of words written and spoken, but in fact could only mutter brokenly. Today I see that my steadfast *desire* was alone responsible for whatever progress or mastery I have made. The reality is always there, and it is preceded by vision. And if one keeps looking steadily the vision crystallizes into fact or deed. There is no escaping it. It doesn't matter what route one travels—every route brings you eventually to the goal. "All roads lead to Heaven," is the Chinese proverb. If one accepted that fully, one would get there so much more quickly. One should not be worrying about the degree of "success" obtained by each and every effort, but only concentrate on maintaining the vision, keeping it pure and steady. The rest is sleight-of-hand work in the dark, a genuine automatic process, no less somnambulistic because accompanied by pains and aches.

Since 11:30 P.M. this evening I've been carried away by the discovery of yellow *ochre!* Marvelous color! I put it in the sky and get dawn, put it in the grass and I get a golden light. Since twilight I've been shuffling back and forth between two water colors—the same theme, different treatment. In each there is a tree (always the same tree, like the one I did in front of St. Augustin's), a body of water—tarn, creek, lake, river??—and hills, green as the hills of Ireland. I used sap green hoping to get a faint gold, but got Irish green instead. A little Prussian blue near the tops of the hills and they glow with all the metallic ores deposited there and guarded by the seven dwarves. Trying to throw the reflection of the hills into the water I had to go over the water so often that there is every kind of blue and green in it. Before going out to the cinema, to see the beloved *Raimu* (the only *human* figure in the movies), I gave the smaller picture a bath. Astonishing effect—and I'm sorry now I went over it again. Everything took on a supernal hue, as at dawn. Where the colors washed out completely it was not just white paper but a wind-swept space in which the vanished colors still spoke faintly. You could see that the hand of man had passed here—like the breath of God moving over the face of the waters. The tree had been smitten by cold blasts. It was wonderful, but like a chump I thought to myself that everybody could see it had been washed—and not made that way by sleight of hand. And finally I got a boat—right shape and right glint fore and aft as she turns with the sun and tide. In the little picture I manage to convey the illusion of two females without (for the first time in my life) putting in hair, eyes, and nose. You can successfully imagine their faces this time. You know they *have* faces! A triumph of the first order! But best of all is the ground—inlaid with yellow ochre so that it gleams in a heavenly way, suggesting not so much "earth" as *the earth*—the earth in some fabled time before the machine was invented. (In the Greek heroic legends, when you think of the battles and the *pourparlers* between the demigods, you conjure up a quite different earth and soil than you get, for example, in a Utrillo or a Cézanne. The earth *was* more golden then, no doubt about it. When a man fell wounded to the earth he felt a kinship with it. There were no shell-holes and gas-eaten grass to sink into. He died in strong sunlight, in a riot of yellow ochre, grass green, chrome yellow, and raw umbers. Or else under a full moon, really *argent* and really swollen to frightening proportions. He saw the trunks of the trees coal black and flecked with silver. He saw in the thick foliage above him a vernal stain in which there were still traces of russet and orange.) Sometimes, in reading a book, you see all these colors again. Sometimes I see it in the movies, leaping out of the black and white film. Tonight, when Raimu was in a rage, his back to the open French window giving out on the Riviera, I saw the most wonderful greens and yellows and wisp-blown foliage and jagged cork-lined trees. And I saw the arm-chair and the sofa with the Matisse wall-paper, the human figures moving in another dimension from the *décor,* and though violent and tragic in their gestures, still not as convincing as the arm-chair, the half-open French window, the serrated and granulated hills, the sword-fish palm leaves, the shrub-stunted olive trees, the quiet heaving bay.

And now I'll tell you a funnier thing still. When I was two-thirds through with my pictures I went back to the studio to have a look at the child's picture I had cut out from that book. And I saw at a glance that "she" knew more about painting than I will ever know. Even when she made the shadow of a swan's long neck in the wrong direction it did not disturb the general air of veracity. What she put down with her brush was absolutely true to her vision. *I* often forget to put in the shadow—until I go to the art gallery and happen to notice that most things cast a shadow. The child is very keenly aware of the aura which surrounds men and things. Grownup children like myself, who are often only addlepated adolescents, forget all about the aura, just as the scientist forgets about the dwarves which inhabit the metals, as Fred says. When I write I am aware of all these things, but when I take up the brush I am so prepossessed with the idea of making something resemble something that I lose track of all reality. My creations, if I can call them that, swim or float or gasp in a vacuum of the senses. Tonight I came closer to this reality than ever before. And I managed it with the *little* brush, which I am usually too impatient to use. I *thought* long about each detail—about the feel of water and the look of hills and how and where the bow of a boat curves. And when the wind sweeps the earth I remembered how it pulls the heavy foliage of the tree, almost as though it would uproot it. I think I conveyed a little of all this in my two long-winded attempts. (Still, when I hang them beside the child's work they are not nearly so good, so honest, so true. The child did not give her picture baths—of that I am certain. And when she made a path in the greensward it *became a path*. Mine are calcimined into the ground.)

But just the same, I praise God for his savin' and keepin' power. I came closer than ever, and I can go to bed with a clear conscience.

But don't forget to see Raimu in *Noix de Coco, drôle de titre! Quand il se met à pleurer, c'est magnifique! C'est un homme, quoi!!!*

Before falling off to sleep last night I ordered my subconscious mind to remember, on waking, the last thought in my head—and it worked. It was to tell you of my impressions on seeing a tiny reproduction in Paris-Soir of a painting by some female artist (perhaps Suzanne Valadon). Looking at the head she had made I was struck by an oft-recurring thought I have when observing heads. It was a head such as only the painters give us; you could not find its counterpart in literature, or even in sculpture. It was—or *is,* because it's an eternal phenomenon in painting—a face dictated by the logic of the brush. From top to bottom the face is foreshortened, and of course correspondingly widened from side to side. You see it most typically, I should say, in Braque's figures. The heads are definitely moulded by the paint to suit the exigencies of the rest of the canvas. The head flows in a sculpturesque way, creating another kind of grace and beauty than that which we are familiar with in life. There is usually a quality of stone-crushed rudeness to the features. When I saw this head in the *rubrique, "A travers les galéries,"* I felt a great joy—partly in recognition of a principle, partly in the discovery of an element which is usually absent from my portraits. If one were to attempt this visage in

water color one would have to do it on moist paper, I
imagine. I intend, by way of beginning, to try it with
powdered crayon, using the fingers for the explosive
quality of bone structure, socket and frontal convolutions.
It is somewhere around the jaw that I feel the keenest
pleasure—hard to describe it, but it is as if the jaw were set
deep back in a widening mound of flesh. It is the carnal
voracity of the mouth and not its verbal facility, or its
"kissability," which gets me. Reichel did one in oil once,
of a medieval German type, in dark olive green with tawny
earth-laden flesh, which haunts me. He gave such a spread
to the face as almost to make it batrachian. It is, however,
a face "for all time," as you said once of Shakespeare's
horses. And there is another thing about these heads—
what I should call the "post-medieval" head. When set
against a landscape or fragment of a landscape (an effect
terrifyingly enhancing, I always think—as though to say .
Man dominating Nature)—the face intuitively reflects
the curves and rhythms of nature. The stark lone head of
modern times is frightening because of the unrelatedness.
It is the symbol of the brain functioning in a void. This
alone is sufficient reason to justify your continued admiration of that French painter whose name I forget—the
one who finally painted with the stump of an arm!
(Renoir) All his women have the quality I speak of. When
we come to Picasso's women we have the flowers of the
machine age, even though they are classified as belonging
to his "classic" period. His massive madonnas are vultures of the great void. Now he is giving them profiles with
a double eye. I don't know the plastic or æsthetic reasons
for these strange apparitions, but I think I detect a
metaphysical reason—and that is, that his women, our
women, have no "etheric" body, so to speak. Being
entirely physical, they become atomic syntheses, imma-
terial conglomerations of electrons, having no real dimen-

sions. Hewed out by the axe, as it were, they are nevertheless impalpable and unsubstantial. The planes which Cézanne discovered fade into Einsteinian abstractions of flesh. They have neither front nor back, and of course no sides. Dali always sees through to the plumbing apparatus. Picasso, being more *Scorpionic,* searches for a more solid substratum, but however frantically he swings the axe his figures are composed on one plane only—and that is cardboard. We have become so accustomed to this cardboard verity that we see nothing unnatural in it. But when we step back a few paces, and look with the eyes of a Renoir, we can discern a tremendous difference.

This is all I have to say, for the moment, about the "broadened" face. I am now going to take a walk through the Parc Montsouris to study the lake, the swans, and the greensward. . . .

Walking along the Boulevard St. Michel tonight studying the reproductions in the windows. Studying eye sockets and lips mostly. Came upon a clump of Renoir women. Discovered all over again the smiling upcurved mouth which enhances the roundness of all his women's faces. A mouth almost like a vagina, if placed Chinese fashion. Decidedly *Renoir* mouths! From this to ancient faces—of every school and age. Examining the modelling employed by various moderns. Cézanne's self-portrait— that slightly bald knob with a sheaf of dandruffy hair falling over his greasy black coat—a hideous portrait, from every standpoint. Absolutely no sense in making self-portraits in such garb and with such uninteresting character. However, the eye sockets interested me. Such a simple technique—yet I miss it constantly. Only this time I saw a little more, saw that he had carried the revolving planes of light and shade into the eye-ball itself, or at any rate into the socket. Going home in the Metro, got so interested in that bit of flesh above the eyeball, in the spaciousness and voluptuousness of it, that I rode past my station. . . . There are several other spots in the human face which are sensually and mysteriously fascinating— the indenture below the nose, the under part of the nose itself, the lobe of the ear, for example. If you begin to concentrate on these you get lost in introspection. The piece of flesh over the eye in a woman can be bewitching. What a big place the eye consumes! I have only recently caught on to that: I am going to increase the prominence of the socket from now on. Noticed too, in my microscopic examinations, that the less the ear is tinkered with the better. So much of the color of life in the face goes dead in the "oriferations" of the ear that unless you use your colors sparingly the ear becomes monstrous. The real tinge of blood, an ebb tinge, as it were, seems to concentrate in the lobe. Right?

Banal deduction, but better late than never. However, thinking of the endless varieties of depicting the face, I got to wondering if you ever thought of lecturing on the various features of the physiognomy, comparing one man's vision or technique with another's. Da Vinci's mouths, as against Rubens', Renoir's, Cézanne's, Picasso's, etc. Botticelli's eyes, as against Cimabue's or Giotto's or Van Gogh's. Perhaps a lot could be said this way—I mean, by the dissection and concentration on single items of the face, rather than the "expression," which is a soul quality and ultimately unanalyzable. I am so thoroughly aware, with writers, of how each one goes about the trick of gesture, conversation, reverie, exclamation, and so on. Herr Peeperkorn's stammer, for example—what a monumental piece of labor! The stammer raised to its ultimate significance. As though Thomas Mann, in sculpturing the human figure, had concentrated all his attention on this one detail, and thereby given us the secret of the man's character.

Yes, I would like to hear you lecture about the face! I ask myself if other men before me have been engrossed by eyeballs or ear lobes. Doubtless they were. Balzac says somewhere, to George Sand, I think it was, how he wrote so and so many bad books, this one to learn French, this one to learn the art of description, this one to learn the knack of conversation, etc. Undoubtedly, anatomists such as Rembrandt, Raphael and Rubens, must also have taken the human figure apart many times and for periods on end seen only this or that which perplexed and intrigued them. Once you begin to concentrate this way, it's amazing what you discover. For, as you well know, you can look at things all your life and not see them really. This "seeing" is, in a way, a "not seeing," if you follow me. It is more of a search for something, in which, being blindfolded, you develop the tactile, the olfactory, the auditory senses—and thus *see* for the first time. One day, odd as it sounds, you suddenly see what makes a wagon for example. You see the wagon in the wagon—and not the cliché image which you were taught to recognize as "wagon" and accept for the rest of your life as a time-saving convenience. The development of this faculty, for an artist in any realm, is what stops the clock and permits him to live fully and freely. He gets out of rhythm with the crowd and in so doing he "creates time" to see what surrounds him. If he were moving (*living!*) like the others he would remain deaf and blind with them. It is the voluntary arrest that really sets him in heavenly motion and permits him to see, feel, hear, think. Eh what?

When I was busy writing *Capricorn* I went dead as regards all these things I now tell you about. It is only now, when my purely critical faculties alone are involved (for my study of Balzac) that the sensuous elements of my being come to life. Now, while I meditate on the phases of Balzac's life, I see with extraordinary relish all the trifling items which go to make up the color and movement of life. Standing before the shop window earlier this evening, I became so engrossed in the shape of a man's lips—the man beside me—that suddenly he became aware of my stare and frowned at me, which woke me up. But looking at those lips I certainly never thought for a moment of the owner of them. They were just lips to me, item no. 946572, in the museum catalogue of Henry Miller lips. They belong more to the shop window than to *Monsieur Tel et Tel*. And more to Giotto, Botticelli, da Vinci, than to the shop window. Finally, pursuing the trend still further, I actually got to imagining the formation of lips in the womb—the whole genetics of lips. And if I had struggled a little more, pehaps I'd have seen the hand of the Creator as he moved over the inchoate flesh and pronounced them to be lips!

And this reminds me that where I so often fail in the water color is in not using the "little" brush, as I remarked before. I should acquire the patience to build up the flesh bit by bit, *feeling* my way along, as I think or sense the meaning of each item in the physiognomy. In oil painting this business of item by item, inch by inch, seems so much more evident. Sometimes I see the whole job as a fine piece of mosaic work, which it is, of course. *Lead and glass,* I often think to myself. No different than a stained glass cathedral window. In Rouault it is pronounced. But with him, the mosaic is so grand and architectural that this pattern-like ant work is lost sight of. I seem to see him pouring the molten glass over the slowly cooling lead. He doesn't wait to get a little slab or globule, but empties the bucket over the face or body or road. He's able to do that, because unlike his *confrères,* he really knows all about stained glass. He's at home with his molten hues and his sombre leads and his iron framework. (I did several heads which people told me later reminded them of Rouault. Small wonder! I remember the moods in which I did these. I remember the bursts of savage freedom.)

In my big Scrap Book, where I occasionally vomit these epileptic fits, I have one especially that I think remarkable. It was unrecognizable for a while, until I got hold of the axe (the "axe" being the crayons) and swung into it with all my muscle and will. The result is a terrifying piece of insanity, regarded exteriorly. In its essence, however, it is a very tender piece of portraiture. It violates all the canons save one—sincerity. It is so earnest and sincere, that if you study it patiently it will make you weep. Because a line, too, if followed back to the original impulse, can reveal all the emotions of the heart. Even when the effect is "cruel," the beat and rhythm of the line reveal the truth of the moment in which it was born. (I am always astonished when people pass ethical judgment on a work. I remember a Frenchman saying to me, when I was making him a gift of one of my best jobs—"Very fine work, yes indeed, but isn't it a bit terrifying?" That query suddenly woke me up to the *external* aspect of the picture, its obvious meaning. I had forgotten all about the subject. I was thinking only of how "successful" it was.)

In Neuilly the other day, attracted by a tiny water color in the window of a book shop. A man in overalls, with fedora and spectacles, wearing huge boots, is standing before the water color muttering and mumbling to himself. I love to listen in on soliloquies, especially *critical* soliloquies. I edged up close to him and watched him intently. He was saying that it was not bad, the *aquarelle*, but very amateurish, unfinished. It was the haste with which it was done that seemed to irritate him. Still looking at the picture, and without putting the question directly to me, he asks, as though still talking to himself (still reflecting on it), whether the "tree" is not too sketchy. (The picture, I must say, was a little scene of the Seine—a scow, a bridge, a tree, a rope—very simple and very adroitly done.) I said aloud, without looking at him, but regarding the picture steadily, "The tree is perfect. The man has said all he wanted to say. It's a tree, and that's enough." Thereupon began a lively discussion about *aquarelles*. The man was a *dealer in pigs* and an amateur collector of *aquarelles*. He bought only what pleased him. But apparently he demanded something more than a five minute sketch. He wanted a tree to have leaves, etc. I repeated that the tree was very obviously a tree, leaves or no leaves. And thereupon I added that I was a painter myself (sic!) and that water colors were my specialty. This provoked a renewed interest on his part. He apologized for being too critical and said what could one expect of a man who is obliged to spend the whole day with pigs. I told him I was delighted to hear this, and that I valued *his* opinion more than that of the critics. That started things. Suddenly, as if by magic, we were talking animatedly, like old friends, about Cézanne, Rouault, Braque, Utrillo, Dostoievski, Hamsun, Francis Carco, Blaise Cendrars, etc. Amazing the things we touched on. Finally he told me how, some twenty years or so ago, he was up in Montmartre one day, and in an art shop he saw some paintings of a man called Utrillo. This man, unknown to him then, had left the paintings to be framed, but not having the money for the frames, was obliged to leave them with the art dealer. He confessed that he was not very much impressed with the paintings, but that a friend who happened to be with him bought the Utrillos and *he* bought some others "which pleased him." The friend, of course, later sold the Utrillos for a good sum. I asked him if he had changed his opinion of Utrillo since, whereupon he said very truthfully and humbly—"No! there is something *sordid* about his pictures which I don't like. I know he is famous now, but that doesn't matter to me." I liked his answer immensely. I told him so. And then, without transition, I launched into a eulogy of Carco's book on Utrillo. I talked about Utrillo as if I knew him intimately. I spoke so convincingly, even in my poor French, that I brought tears to the eyes of this dealer! But what got me was this—the word *"souffrance"* had stirred something in him. He couldn't get over it. *"Souffrance"* explained everything. *"Ecoutez, monsieur,"* he said, *"moi je ne suis qu'un ignorant, un sacré marchand de cochons, mais j'ai vécu . . . j'ai mes experiences de la vie . . . j'ai souffert. La vie d'un artiste, surtout la vie d'un peintre, n'est qu'un Calvaire. Ce que vous dites, monsieur, me touche profondémente. Je m'excuse d'avoir fait la critique d'une oeuvre qui est probablement au-dessus de ma compréhension. Moi, je ne suis qu'un amateur. J'aime les aquarelles. Je les garde chez moi pour le simple plaisir de les contempler. C'est curieux, mais c'est la vérité. Si vous avez du temps, monsieur, je vous invite à m'accompagner pour que je puisse vous montrer ma petite collection . . ."* And so I went with him and I saw his collection. And I had a couple of cognacs with him and we wept together, the pork dealer and I, over the crucifixion of the artist. A wonderful day! All due to a *Monsieur Asselin, peintre, que je ne connais pas. Vive Monsieur Asselin! Vive l'aquarelle! Vive les marchands de cochons! Par un beau jour, l'aquarelle, même celle d'un inconnu, peut ouvrir les portes du Paradis. Vive la Seine, et la chalande qui passe sous les ponts! Vive l'arbre, sans ou avec feuilles! Vive le soleil! Vive Asselin!*

The opposite of this is an experience with a fat female clerk at the Post Office. Curious about a roll of water colors I was dispatching for my show in Washington, and it being just around Xmas, I impulsively offered to do a water color for her while in London. I felt sorry for her, sitting behind the bars all day, glueing stamps to other people's letters. *Eh bien,* I gave her one on my return from London. She was absent that day, so I left it for her with the *chef du bureau.* A few days later I arrived and greeted her. She barely greeted me. I waited until she had stamped my things, waited while she made change, waited, waited . . . and not a word out of her regarding the *aquarelle.* Finally I thought to myself—perhaps the *chef* forgot to give it to her. "Did you get the aquarelle I left the other day?" I asked as I was making ready to go. She looked at me coldly, dropped her eyes, and said in an irritated manner: *"L'aquarelle? Oui, oui, on me l'a donnée. Oui!" Et c'était tout!* I turned on my heel and walked away. I walked around the block three times, debating whether to go back and ask her what the hell she meant by such insolence *or* give me back my aquarelle! I was furious. Finally I closed the matter in my mind by calling her a *"vieux con, une salope, un chou, une branleuse, une grosse légume, une abrutie . . ."*

The *aquarelle* was a bit mysterious, I'll admit. You couldn't tell whether it was two birds fighting in the dark or a waterfall in sunlight. For me it was very clear: it was "light and dark," the confluence of all the juxtapositions of color. The *carrefour* of twilight, or—just a "glassy wet fart," if you like. But how explain such subtleties to an ignoramus? And in bad French! I gave it up. Spent the rest of the day conjugating French verbs, making genders, choosing elegant, cynical, sinister subjunctives. My water colorist's heart was wounded to the core. It was a royal setback. *Mieux vaut un marchand de cochons! Si je ne suis pas un Asselin je suis tout de même un Henri Miller. J'ai du coeur, quoi! Je suis un sensible. C'est une sacrée vie, cette vie sacrée d'un peintre...*

Sunday, March 12, 1939
2:00 A.M.

Emil, I must get this down before going to bed or I never will. An evening with my friend, "the Aztec," as I call him. Here in the studio. At dinner he begins talking, as he often does, about the period just after the war. "L'époque bohème." I can't give it to you in an orderly fashion. Suffice it to indicate the highlights. It's a good note to close this little book on, because it's extremely human and perhaps not a little sad.

As I've told you before, this friend of mine was intimately associated with the poets and painters of the period. He was himself a painter, a bad one, I gather. He came out of the war in a trance-like state, too deeply shocked by all he had experienced to recapture the gayety of youth. He counted as his friends such figures as Blaise Cendrars, Max Jacob, Kisling, Leger, André Salmon. He was a *copain* of Modigliani, Apollinaire, Vlaminck, Picasso, Derain, Braque, Juan Gris, Diego Rivera and others.

What started the conversation this evening was a remark which he let drop about Picasso and the origin of Cubism. He practically gave me the day and hour of its birth. The sudden transition from the Blue period to the African. The curious concidence between Picasso's intellectual *floraison* and the treatments he was receiving for some mysterious ailment. A vivid picture in my brain of Picasso seated at the old Rotonde with the others— neither jovial nor glum, but a bit detached. Drinking only Vittel.

To proceed more rapidly, because I can give you only the highlights... Vlaminck is then a bicycle rider, a man of the country, "a tender one," always talking about painting with his guts. Derain is already fat, extremely well read, a terrific drinker, charming, and all that. Apollinaire is the *metteur-en-scène*. Max Jacob, always the buffoon and the wit, is also the kind-hearted Jew who takes Picasso's work and, harnessing himself to a push-cart, makes the rounds of Paris trying to sell Picasso's canvases.

There are reunions in the rue Ravignan where Picasso then worked and slept—just above the Place des Abbesses, Montmartre. You probably remember the spot. Juan Gris is there—handsome, intellectual, rather *sec*. Diego Rivera also, who is soon to do the most wonderful imitations of Picasso's cubistic paintings. He has an Arabian beard, an air of Toledo. (A little later, at the beach at Arcachon, he will give milk—when the moon is full.)

Then Bougival . . . the outdoor banquets by the Seine, the discussions about Negro sculpture, the primitives, mythology and so on. Derain perhaps the most sensitive of all. Braque applying himself to the theories in intellectual fashion. Vlaminck pounding his chest and bellowing like an ox. Everything is in the bag. It needs only a touch of genius to explode the magazine. And of course Picasso does it!

To me it was all like a description of worlds in process of birth. (Does not everything happen in flashes, in moments of inspiration?)

Soutine also enters the picture. The boon companion of Modigliani who, up until his third or fourth apéritif, is brilliant and entertaining—after that a madman, *un exalté*. (Soutine is now quietly living below me, with his new red-haired model, a "Soutine" in every respect. He seems tame now, as if trying to recover from the wild life of other days. Hesitates to salute you in the open street, for fear you will get too close to him. When he opens his trap it's to say how warm or how cold it is—and does the neighbor's radio bother you as it does him?)

Anyway, the period in question is still one of real camaraderie, of reunions, of feasting and drinking. When it is too cold to work one digs up a few bottles of *vin rouge*, locks the door, and goes to bed with the model. For months after the war my friend continued to wear the uniform which was too small for him—no money for civilian clothes. Now and then there was a sensational duel, over some trifle, followed by a lively banquet and a boost in the price of paintings (for those involved). Some grew wealthy over-night, and of course quickly forgot about their more unfortunate comrades. Max Jacob seeks a retreat in a monastery where he will continue to paint and write. And this reminds me of a line I stumbled on recently, from Chesterton's book on St. Francis of Assisi: "It was in fact his (St. Francis') whole function to tell men *to start afresh* and, in that sense, to tell them to forget."

All of them, from Cendrars on down, had a terrible baptism in the war. Cendrars, the eternal adventurer, has to learn how to do things all over again—with his left hand. Their whole world is smashed. Their best friends are dead, their ambitions nipped in the bud. Yet, as I listen to all this, I realize that for most of them the catastrophe served to augment their human qualities. They sound "tender" compared with the generation of today. Now they are dispersed, each one famous in his way, each one working alone, indifferent perhaps to the fate of the others.

In his long monologue this evening my friend brought them all to life for me—and the epoch and the climate. Speaking of Paris, the changing Paris he has known, speaking of the "greys" which make Paris, he says: "It requires a long education to appreciate the nuances of grey . . . *c'est toute une histoire.*" How true! From Paris to Istanbul, Morocco, Toledo, and always the "values" of each clime, each scene. Then back to Paris, to that sombre hue which at first seems sordid—until one begins to recognize here and there, little by little, the nuances of grey. From the "greys" he goes into a eulogy of Léon Paul-Fargue's poetry. "The master of greys," he calls him. "The magician of nuances." I know what he means. I know what a magician Paul-Fargue is. To read him makes me tongue-tied.

From the magician to the "mage"—*Balzac!* The esoteric doctrine. The religion of the magi. In his vest pocket my friend always carries the little fetish containing those same precious gifts which the Three Wise Men from the East once brought with them. He burns a tiny bit of myrrh for me, to give me an idea of what is meant by "the odor of sanctity." With it a discourse on the doctrine of Unity, as revealed by Claude Saint-Martin, *"le philosophe inconnu". En passant* a "profile" of Jolas looking towards the source of the Rhine, undecided whether he is a Field-Marshal or a reincarnation of Wotan. Between times making cryptic references to Paracelsus' thaumaturgy and the real meaning of the philosopher's stone. Asking me abruptly to find out for him all I can about the mystery of Mesa Verde. (Balzac too was mad about the Indians!) Would I care to see some Mayan alphabets? Showing me thereupon the lost continents— on my map in the studio. Explaining why he believes there was a green or a blue race of men as well as red, brown, yellow, black and white.

And me saying—"*Pourquoi pas?*" Which is exactly what started us off earlier in the evening. It was this expression of Picasso's which had set me going. *Pourquoi pas?* to everything!

Who is the man who triumphs? The one who *believes.* Let the "intelligent" ones doubt, criticize, categorize and define. The man of heart believes. And the world belongs to him who believes most. Nothing is too silly, too trivial, too far-fetched or too stupendous for man to believe. Learning crushes the spirit; belief opens one up, delivers one. When I listen to my friend I sometimes wonder what people would say if they could hear what passes between us. He has never said anything, let me tell you, too fantastic for me to swallow. From poetry and painting to mythology or alchemy, from the mundane to the sublime hierarchies, it all makes one to me, and sense too. Profound sense.

It is getting late and I am weary. But I thought you would relish getting a whiff of this talk-fest. Often during the evening I thought of Reichel whose glass mystery hangs just behind me. He too belongs to this world of magic and mystery. He comes no more, Reichel, but his spirit is here—and his pictures talk incessantly. I think of him on his weekly visits to Notre Dame, entering by the Porte Astrologique and mounting to the tower *"to feel the chimères,"* as he says. Then descending to leave by the Porte Chimique. But always hoping that one day they will open the Porte Magique for him. Reichel, incidentally, has a mortal fear of decomposing into "a chemical fluid" when he dies. Does not want to be corked up in a bottle. Has a dread of being "misused." But all of this more another time . . .

"It makes fun," as Reichel used to say. But it's getting late. Tonight I will sleep with the stars, the symbols, the fluids and the dreams of another epoch. *Je me griserai avec les paroles des poètes maudits. Vive la magie! Vive le magisme! Bonne nuit!*

POSTSCRIPTUM

After eating a bit of ginger from Hong Kong, after preparing the glass slab with colors, after buying a palette knife, I settle down to my first *gouache.* From now on I'm going to paint for myself—decorate my own walls.

But first a coda to the Picasso business. It was while taking the injections that Picasso, who had now begun to paint in earnest, gave himself up to night work. In the morning his friends would find the paintings lying on the floor.

That's all! *The Night Life!*

Reflections on the MAURIZIUS CASE

(A humble appraisal of a great book)

Henry Miller

1974

This novel* by one of Germany's great writers is based on a famous miscarriage of justice which, like our own Sacco and Vanzetti case, had repercussions throughout the world.

With that fullness and depth of insight which distinguishes the creative artist, Wassermann expanded the theme to a degree which gives it the magnitude of a Greek tragedy.

Etzal Andergast, a boy of sixteen, plays a singular and most disturbing role in this drama of conflicting passions. It is through his fanatical belief in, and pursuit of, justice that the condemned Maurizius, who has already spent eighteen years in the penitentiary, is released.

The book offers no balm, no solutions. All the characters involved in the affair suffer tragic fates with the exception of Anna Jahn who had committed the murder for which Maurizius was unjustly punished. Etzel, the hero of the book, is definitely blighted by his experience. Maurizius himself, shortly after his release, commits suicide. Etzel's father who as prosecuting attorney was responsible for the

---

*The Maurizius Case by Jacob Wassermann, translated by Caroline Newton and published by Horace Liveright, New York, 1929.

injustice done Maurizius, goes completely to pieces.

A grim and grisly story shot through with lurid flashes which reveal the heights and depths of the German soul awaiting the advent of a leader who will bring about its dissolution.

The action takes place in the town of Hanau principally, and in Berlin, where Etzel tracks down Waremme; also in the penitentiary at Kressa near Hanau, where Maurizius is imprisoned.

The story opens eighteen years after the famous crime has occurred. We follow the incidents leading up to the shooting of Maurizius' wife through the eyes and lips of the various characters—Maurizius himself, Waremme-Warschauer, old man Maurizius, and others. Everything hinges on the false testimony of Waremme, the close friend of Maurizius. Who did the shooting remains a mystery until almost the end.

The boy Etzel, who is obsessed with Maurizius' innocence, seems to be motivated by a higher sense of duty and justice than his inflexible father who, in his personification of the law, takes on the proportions of a monster. But in reality, though the boy is unaware of it, his chivalrous deed is prompted by a spirit of vengeance: he wants to destroy his father's work. In the back of his mind is the obscure feeling that his father is responsible for everything. Deprived of his mother's affection he turns into an avenger. In seeking the liberation of the innocent victim, Maurizius, he is unconsciously seeking the liberation of his mother, who, like the prisoner, has been made to suffer unjustly at the hands of the father.

The theme of the story is not alone the inadequacy of human justice, but the impossibility of ever attaining it. All the characters testify to this, in their own way, even that "Pillar of Justice," Herr Von Andergast himself. Justice, it appears, is merely a pretext for inflicting cruelty upon the weaker one. *Justice, divorced from love, becomes revenge.*

Around the figure of Maurizius, whose weakness of character precipitates the crime, revolves as in a whirlpool a veritable constellation of figures whose motives, passions and interests are inextricably interwoven. The question of justice, which is the underlying theme, is practically smothered by the wealth of subsidiary drama engendered by what might be called fate.

Some of the most illuminating, as well as harrowing, scenes take place in the penitentiary during the conversations between Maurizius and Baron Von Andergast, and between Maurizius and an old prison-keeper named Klakusch.

"When alone," says Maurizius, "a human being has no soul . . . And consequently, alone, he has no God . . . for me no one dies."

The dialogues with Klakusch, who is a Dostoievskian sort of figure, the voice of conscience itself, are particularly revelatory. They touch the limits of human understanding. For example, about this question of justice . . .

"What do you mean, *justice?*" says Maurizius.

"No one should really use that word," answers Klakusch.
"Why, Klakusch?"

"It is a word like a fish, it slips away from one when one seizes it." Then he adds: "If one had the voice, what could not one attain? But the voice is lacking."

In speaking of Klakusch to Herr Andergast, Maurizius remarks: "There was something remarkable about the man. He pretended to be so simple, he seemed so harmless and when one had been with him awhile, one had the feeling that he knew about everything in the world and one merely needed to ask him about it. But he was only interested in the penitentiary; he talked of nothing but the convicts. . ."

"I can tell you what a criminal is," said Klakusch one day. "A criminal is one who ruins himself, that's what he is. The human being who ruins himself is a criminal."

On another occasion Klakusch says to Maurizius: "I'd like to know why you're always so sad. I always say to the boys: 'Everything's regulated for you, you have a good bed, sufficient nourishment, have a roof over your heads—what more do you want? No worries, no business, don't have to struggle —what more do you want?' "

After a remark or two by Maurizius, Klakusch continues: "But realize this, the judge can't do differently. The mistake is this: When a judge condemns he, as a human being, is condemning a human being and that should not be."

"Really," says Maurizius, astonished, "do you think that that must not be?"

"It must not be," repeats Klakusch in an unforgettable tone. "A human being should not condemn a human being."

"And what about punishment?" Maurizius replies, "Isn't punishment necessary? It has been since the world began."

Klakusch leans over Maurizius and whispers: "Then we must destroy the world and create people who think differently.* That has been hammered into us since childhood but it has nothing to do with real human beings. It's a lie, that's what it is. A lie. He who punishes lies away his own sin. There you have it. . ."

Pursuing the subject further, Maurizius tries to point out (Maurizius, the condemned man, no less!) that society had gotten away from the real principle of punishment long ago, as well as from the principle of retaliation; the protection of society and the improvement of the criminal was the only concern. "Klakusch," he says, "held that the initiated simply laughed at the idea of either protection or improvement; how was one to keep an insane person from lacerating his face with his own hands? The world of human beings was such an insane person; it pretends to protect what it

*Italics mine

constantly destroys by its lack of understanding. For this reason Klakusch said: '*Stop, world of humans, and attack the problem from a different angle!*' "

Finally we come to this amazing *déroulement*, as narrated by Maurizius to Attorney-General Andergast. What follows is given immediately after the above citation. . . .

"We had this conversation one December afternoon; since morning the fall of snow had been darkening the cell and before he left Klakusch said: 'I don't enjoy things any more, my days are full and over. I know too much about things, nothing more can go into my head or my heart.' When he came back again towards evening to empty the bucket—he always did it for me, though according to the regulations of the house, I should have done it myself—as he stood there before me, I summoned my courage and asked him: 'Tell me, Klakusch, do you think that there are innocent people sentenced in this house?' He seemed unprepared for the question and answered hesitantly: 'That might well be.' I continued my questioning: 'How many innocent people who have been condemned have you known during your work, I mean, known as guiltless?' He considered a while, then he counted on his fingers, murmuring the names in low tones. 'Eleven.'

" 'And did you at once believe in their innocence when you first came to know them?' 'No, not that,' he replied, 'not that; if one believed in their innocence and then had to watch them eating their hearts out, if one were certain, then, I say. . .' I urged him on: 'Then, what then, Klakusch?'

" 'Well, then,' he said, 'then, speaking strictly, one could not continue to live.' It had already become dark in my cell, I could still just perceive his figure, so I ventured the question which I had on my heart and which I wanted to utter. 'Well, how do matters stand with me, do you consider me guilty or innocent?' And he: 'Must I answer?'

" 'I should be glad if you would answer me openly and

candidly,' I said. He considered again, then he said: 'Right, tomorrow morning you shall have your answer.' And early the next day came the answer. He had hanged himself from the window-frame of his room."

This indeed might well be the author's own answer to the enigma, one feels. For, as the story unrolls, as the dark strands in which the crime is knotted are undone, each of the characters involved, from the iron-clad prosecuting attorney down to the weak Maurizius, even to Etzel the deliverer, are seen to be equally guilty. Society itself is arraigned: we are all stained with guilt. That seems to be the author's point of view. And therefore there can be no solution, no end to crime, no end to man's injustice to man except through the tedious and painful increase of understanding, sympathy and forbearance. In trying to fix the responsibility, in searching for the motive and the cause of crime, we sink into a bog from which there seems to be no possibility of extrication. All is illusion and delusion. There is no firm ground on which to stand. Crime and punishment are rooted in the very fibre of man's being. Even the lovers of justice— perhaps especially the lovers of justice—stand condemned before the higher tribunal of love and mercy.

Little Etzel Andergast, whom Wassermann pictures as a David battling against Goliath, and who seems the very incarnation of justice, is a figure worthy of the most serious study. As the sequels to *The Maurizius Case* reveal* the author seems to have been baffled by his own creation. He died before he was able to give us the final book which would expose the full nature of this enigmatic creature. There is something monstrous about Etzel Andergast: he is fascinatingly attractive and repellent at the same time. He

*Doctor Kerkhoven (or Etzel Andergast in the German) and Kerkhoven's Third Existence.
**Pages 316 to 321 of Doctor Kerkhoven.

stands for the new type of youth which made possible the advent and sway of an Adolf Hitler. He might even be regarded as an embryonic Hitler. He is "the murderer of the soul," to use the language of his victims.

In the second volume of the trilogy Wassermann gives a rather spacious summary of *The Maurizius Case* in order to throw further light on the baleful character of young Etzel Andergast.** Once again we shudderingly observe the effect upon Etzel of the news that Maurizius was pardoned. "Can they throw him (Maurizius) a wretched alms instead of paying him what they owe?" he screams. At this point the world becomes for Etzel chaos; there is no longer sense to anything. Justice, he believes, demands not that Maurizius be pardoned but that the State, or society, beg forgiveness of Maurizius. What Etzel expected was not only complete exoneration of the innocent victim but the exposure and punishment of all who contributed to the man's needless persecution and suffering. Completely balked and frustrated, in the end as in the beginning, by his father's acts, the boy is transformed into a raving fury. As once he was cheated of his mother's affection so now he is robbed of his triumph. With such a background anything may be expected when a character of this sort comes to maturity. Given the poper conditions, he is capable of shaking the world to its foundation. And who will remember, when this incredible demon rides the whirlwind, that as a boy he was the very symbol of righteousness?

Whether the author intended it or not, it is obvious that the most amazing parallels can be drawn between the plight of Germany, as Hitler saw it, and the plight of Maurizius, as Etzel Andergast saw it.

One of the most obscure and yet significant details, with regard to Etzel's activity in the Maurizius affair, is the involuntary coupling in his own mind of the criminal and his own mother. As Wassermann himself puts it, "only a dark yearning persists in him, as the image of his mother gradually fades from memory, and in some strange way this yearning becomes mingled with the news of the murdered Maurizius, as though, from that quarter also, innocence had sent out her ghostly messengers." Back of the desire to rescue and absolve the innocent Maurizius lies the secret longing to liberate and rejoin his mother. The mystery which enwraps his distant mother is of the same texture as that which envelops the unhappy victim languishing in the penitentiary. Fate has conspired against them both. But as Etzel proceeds with his investigations, the logic of circumstances tends more and more to corroborate his intuitions, namely, that it is his father who is at the bottom of all this horrible injustice. In a letter which he writes to his mother, but which he is unable to post because he does not know her address, he says: "A boy my age seems to have his hands and feet bound with stout ropes. Who knows, perhaps when the string is once cut, one is already lame and tame. That is probably the purpose. One is to be tamed. Have they made you tame also?* . . . I would so much like to know what's the matter. I know you understand me. I have the feeling that you have had an injustice done you. Is that so? . . . *You must know that injustice to me is the most horrible thing in the world.** I can't give you any idea of my feelings when I experience injustice, whether towards myself or others; it's just the same. It goes right through me. It makes my body and soul ache, it is as if one had poured my mouth full of sand and I must choke on the spot."

Why this ingrained, obsessive hatred of injustice in a mere lad of sixteen? Obviously only one reason: the loss of his mother's affection. Who is responsible for this deprivation? Obviously that tyrannical monster, his father. "In his capac-

---

*One thinks of Kierkegaard's parable of The Wild Goose.
**Italics mine

ity of magician (that is to say, in his role of chief thwarter and stifler), Etzel had given him the name of Trismegistus. Always when he thought of his father in his punitive function he called him so." The amputation, then, of the boy's affective nature made him, so to speak, lop-sided. Unable to give expression to the normal instinct to love, he could assert himself only through rebellion. To save Maurizius is tantamount to saving himself. Impossible to live in this world as an amputated, crippled being: the father's crippling influence must be destroyed, injustice must be wiped out.

Needless to point out, we have here the crux of Etzel's dilemma. The fight against injustice, the desire to overthrow the established order, the very instinct to rebel, so fundamental in the human heart, is revealed as ambivalence. What Etzel demands, what the world of suffering millions demand, though they know not how to voice it, is not the elimination of injustice nor even the establishment of justice, but the satisfaction of a hunger more imperious still, because it is a positive and permanent need of the human heart. This is nothing less than the condition of love. Whoever is denied his rightful share of love is crippled and thwarted in the very roots of his being. No matter how noble the cause, no matter how bright the banner under which he fights, no matter if God Himself seems to be on his side, he who seeks merely to eradicate injustice is enacting a travesty. The inflated ego, drunk with power, knows no bounds: the end is self-destruction. In the tyrant it is easy enough to follow the play of this dire logic, but in the righteous and indignant ones the drama has even more disastrous repercussions. The Etzels of this world, and they are to be found on both sides of the fence, can have no rest, can know no peace. Though they pose as the saviours of the innocent, they succeed only in bringing about destruction. They are the self-deluders, and the very passion which wings them on their way is a poison to the world. This seems to be the gist of Wassermann's message.

When Etzel runs away to Berlin, in order to track down the perjurer, Waremme, he leaves a note for his father wherein he says: "I am quite conscious of what I owe you. But we have no access with one another and it is useless for me to look for any. *I cannot say that anything stands between us because everything stands between us. . .** The truth must come to light. I wish to find the truth. . ." And then, in classic manner, begins the voyage which ends in a circle. It is the old, old story of the hero setting forth on the compulsive errand of adventure to liberate the fancied victim of injustice and thus overthrow the powers that be. In the name of truth and justice he becomes himself an agent of crime. In this case, as we have observed, the victim of injustice, Maurizius, appears to be invested with a greater sense of clarity and enlightenment that his would-be saviour. By his suffering he attains a degree of wisdom which is denied his liberator. His salvation, we discover, did not lie in the attainment of his rightful freedom but in the atonement of his sins. Though actually it was not he who killed his wife, but his sister-in-law, Anna Jahn, it was the sense of his own guilt which forced him to become the scapegoat. In his heart, he admits, he had been guilty of killing his wife. Maurizius is highly aware of the fact that it is his own conscience which has imposed the extreme punishment he is obliged to endure. That eighteen years later, when liberated from his cell, he should seek out Anna Jahn and discover her to be empty and worthless, seems on the surface to be a gratuitious insult at the hands of fate, but closer examination of his character merely reveals how natural and fitting this dénouement is. It was in the hope of finding a ballast, a rudder, an anchorage, that Maurizius had allied himself with a woman fifteen

---

*Italics mine

years his senior. The spoiled child quickly becomes the older woman's darling. He looks for support without, and not within. When he finds himself confronted with the young sister, who because of her age, her charm, her beauty, is capable of inspiring true love, he is at a loss what to do. He would like to throw away the crutch which has served him, but he is already too beholden to this crutch of a wife, too conscience-stricken to abdicate. The truth is that he needs them both—and that is impossible, at least in our society.

Anna Jahn no one thought of suspecting, except old father Maurizius. To the world, as the trial dragged on, Anna Jahn assumed more and more the character of a spotless angel. The darkness which surrounds her actions, even her motivations, can only be understood in the light of her relationship with Gregor Waremme, alias Warschauer. But of this more later. . . .

Waremme is a powerful figure, Satanic really, who as Wassermann so justly puts it has betrayed every true instinct. A renegade in the deepest sense of the word. Born a Jew, he becomes an ardent Catholic, a German nationalist, a warmonger. Gifted by nature with a diversity of talents, by his magnetism capable of exerting tremendous influence over others, he nevertheless creates nothing but tragedy about him. When Etzel encounters him he is in the last stages of disintegration, a fact which in no wise minimizes his seductive powers. Indeed it is only Etzel's innocence which saves him from being devoured by this sinister figure. It is as though a roué were to fall hopelessly in love with a girl of virginal purity. Waremme has no defense against innocence. The scenes between these two in the shabby purlieus of Berlin smack of the legendary encounter between Theseus and the Minotaur in the heart of the labyrinth.

I said a while back that the hero of the book is Etzel Ander-gast. If we employ the term hero in the superficial sense he is. And Gregor Waremme is then the villain. But since, in a book of the scope and profundity indicated there can be no hero-villain antagonism, since all the leading characters are both hero and villain combined, I prefer to regard Waremme as the leading figure.

Originally I had undertaken a study of this book to make a working script of it for the films. I wanted more than any one on earth to see this story portrayed on the screen. I wanted it to reach every home. I wanted to see results—I mean, for the men behind bars throughout the civilized world. I wanted what Etzel wanted, namely, the liberation of the innocent. Only, to my way of thinking, all who were behind bars were innocent!

Oddly enough, I fell into the same trap as Etzel. Despite all reason, I too wanted to see the world shaken to its foundations on this question of injustice. A lifetime of disappointing experiences did not prevent me from hoping and praying that this particular story would find its mark—and perhaps alter the human heart.

Here I must admit that I was incompetent to make the necessary script. Meanwhile the war was increasing in magnitude. To make a film about injustice one would have to draw a blue-print of the cosmos. The world, like a ripe cheese, was crawling with Mauriziuses. Everywhere injustice was rampant. The very term "prisoner" had become almost

meaningless; where formerly there were thousands now there
were hundreds of thousands, millions, in fact. Prisoners of
war, to be sure, but prisoners none the less, and most of them
suffering a more horrible fate than the fictive Maurizius.
Flesh and blood prisoners, releasable, if they survived, after
the war. A difference there to be sure, but who would bother
now to ponder that difference? To divert attention to that
other type of prisoner, the convict, might be regarded as a
betrayal. The war comes first! Win the war (both sides saying
the same thing, of course), and we'll take care of the other
injustices. But will they? The triumphs and defeats of war are
scarcely calculated to soften men's hearts. The victims of
society's injustice will be forgotten after the war, as they have
been during and before the war. Everybody knows that. What
to do, then? There seems to be only one logical answer.
"Destroy the world and create people who think differently!"

And that is what Wassermann, in this trilogy which centers about Etzel Andergast and Dr. Kerkhoven, seems to be
concerned with: the destruction of our present world and
the emergence of a new and better type of human being. The
liberated Maurizius was incapable of starting a new life.
Nearly everyone now behind bars is incapable of starting a
new life. So are the jailers, the judges, the lawyers who
prosecuted or defended them. Society itself, the kind of
society we believe in, at least, is hog-tied. It refuses to con-
done and it refuses to beg forgiveness. By exercising the
prerogative of punishment it has brought itself before the
tribunal of justice. Such a society inevitably brings about its
own end.

No, society can furnish no solution, because from top to
bottom it is permeated with wrong principles, wrong motives.
Philosophers, artists, statesmen, scientists, how many of them
have depicted our ignominious end! We pay no heed. It
would not matter if every hour of the day and night, from

every radio station in the civilized world, we blasted dire warning. We would still be unable to do anything. The script writer who blithely altered the book to suit the needs of the screen—and thus fattened his own pocket book—is a symbol of the great majority who make up our kind of society.

Truth is unimportant, justice is unimportant. What is important is that "we carry on." "Business as usual," no matter where it leads us. Give us any kind of trash, but keep the cinemas going!

Even Waremme, diabolical figure that he is, is leagues above this plane of thinking. Waremme capitulates to the world, but only as a giant bends to the ropes which pull him down. Waremme is not of the world, any more than Etzel or Maurizius. That is why the book will always be infinitely superior to any film interpretation of it that may be made. There are no figures in the cinema world capable of registering the thoughts and feelings of these chief characters. Even were they to mouth the author's very lines they would remain unconvincing. To understand and enjoy this drama, as Wassermann portrayed it, society would have to be something other than it now is. Wassermann is already talking to a higher society, a better society. He assumes that we have ears to hear with, that we have eyes, and heart. But in our society these organs are missing. Ours is already a society of "gueules cassées," a society of deaf, halt, blind, diseased— and faceless ones. The blind lead the blind. We are pouring over the cliff. Those who are able to read and understand are going over the cliff too, make no mistake about it. The message is not for us. The message is wasted. It is already too late. The prison walls are being laid low, but so are the inmates. And we are all inmates of the same prison. We are all being blown up together. Hurrah! Hoorah!

Too late, Klakusch. Too late to pay heed to those wondrous words of yours.

"STOP, WORLD OF HUMANS, AND ATTACK THE PROBLEM FROM A DIFFERENT ANGLE!"

To whom did you address those words? Not to us. We are deaf. We are going over, like the Gadarene swine. No stopping us. Hooray! Hurrah!

I have pondered over *The Maurizius Case* more than over any book I have ever read, I guess, unless it be *William Blake's Circle of Destiny*.* I forget about it for a while and then it comes back, insistently and insidiously. I talk about it to every one who seems to lend a willing ear. I see from the faces of my listeners it cannot possibly have the same meaning for them which it has for me. It is one of those books which seems to have been written expressly for the one who is reading it. Nothing can explain its seduction. It is not the greatest book I have ever read, nor the best written. Neither is its theme the highest. It is a piece of propaganda to which a man like myself is peculiarly susceptible. It haunts me, as the Sphinx haunted the men of old. For it does contain a secret in the form of a riddle. It is mysterious in that despite all explanations, those of the author, those of the interpreters of it, nothing is truly explained. Is it because it is about justice, of which we know almost nothing? Is it because the description of human justice awakens in us intimations of a divine justice? Why does such a knight errant as Etzel develop later into a veritable monster? Does it mean that the man who is overly concerned about justice is himself the most unjust of men? Is it man's business to mete

---

*By Milton O. Percival (Columbus University Press.)

out justice here on earth? And if he does not attempt to do so, is he thereby shirking a duty towards his fellow-man, or is he inspiring him to a higher attitude? Klakusch is so terribly right in his view—at least I feel so—and yet he is a minor figure in the book, an incidental one, a pathetic, almost ludicrous one. Without Klakusch, the victim Maurizius would have had nothing, no one, to sustain him. Klakush has to kill himself in order to convince Maurizius of the truths he utters. The world will never "tackle the problem from a different angle." From the world level every problem is insuperable; the angles of approach are always from below, from men submerged. The death of Klakusch serves no purpose apparently. (Unless it affects men like me.) Those who have the power to open the doors will keep them closed until the crack of doom. They will drag the world down with them rather than change their attitude.

I made mention earlier of the fact that the author had stressed the connection, in Etzel's mind, between the prisoner Maurizius and the mother whom he had been robbed of. I come back to this again. To liberate the mother! It has only one meaning for me—to liberate his own power to love. To save Maurizius really means nothing. Etzel never knew the man. He is for him, as he was for his father before him, "a case." He is the excuse which Etzel needs in order to revenge himself upon the father. Why does he fly into such a rage when he learns that Maurizius has been released? (The release meant only that he had been "pardoned.") Had the man's freedom been his sole concern, as it would be if one acted from ordinary human motives, he would have been happy, even if not entirely satisfied with his father's actions or motives. But it is not Maurizius he is concerned about—it is this abstract thing, justice. *Is it, however?* Is it justice he wants in fullest measure, or is it that lost twin of justice—love? It is he, Etzel, who has been cheated, not Maurizius.

It is in the second volume of the trilogy, *Dr. Kerkhoven*, that we perceive with horror how distorted has become Etzel's love. Here begins the enigma of another triangular affair, one in which Etzel behaves very much like the Maurizius whom he tried to succor. I mean, to use Wassermann's own words when referring to Maurizius, that "he is not man enough to give up one thing or the other." "Renunciation," says Wassermann, "requires a clear recognition; but such half-baked characters (as Maurizius) are seldom clearly aware of their situations or of their secret impulses; they prefer to flounder about in uncertainty."

The difference between the two cases, however, is that Maurizius was merely a "weak" man. Etzel is positively evil. He has not only betrayed himself, he betrays his saviour, Dr. Kerkhoven. It is interesting to note, in this connection, that the woman in the triangle, Marie, the wife of Kerkhoven, is a woman somewhat older than Etzel. Can it be that in his twisted brain she has replaced the mother whose love he was denied? His passion for Marie is uncontrollable. There is something desperate about it, something almost ferocious. Etzel, like Maurizius, is to be pitied, not censured. We know that he does not *wish* to dishonour the man he reveres, Dr. Kerkhoven. He is compelled to do so by forces beyond him. But he is guilty, we feel, and towards Maurizius we are not inclined to feel thus. His acts are all violations, that is it. He makes us recoil in horror and dismay. He makes even the great, saintly figure, Kerkhoven, lust to murder. And we applaud Kerkhoven. We know that he is justified in wishing Etzel dead.

The Mother! One must bear in mind that the picture of her had been completely erased from his memory. "He has no picture of her, not even an internal one, since it is so long since she has disappeared out of his life, and every memory of her, for some reason that he cannot understand, has been

obliterated, even all external marks, photographs, portraits."
Wassermann dwells frequently on the antagonisms in the
home, as though to put his finger on the source of all future
troubles. Referring to one of Etzel's playmates in whose home
there is no peace, he observes: "The revolutionary attitude
of a boy often has its roots in a disorderly household. In
many bourgeois homes affection has been dead for generations. A heart must be rarely gifted if an unsatisfied hunger
for affection is not to make it thirst for revenge." And later,
when the teacher Camill Raff endeavors to analyze Etzel's
strange behaviour, when he sets to pondering over the meaning of that peculiar question Etzel had put to him—"Are
there conflicting duties, or is there only one duty?"—he
ruminates thus: "A sixteen year old boy must resolve freely,
must move in the illusion of infinity. If he is compelled to
give up the freedom of dream and play for the paths of
purpose and utility, suffering inevitably commences because
he soon senses and comes to realize that he is being forced
to give up a happy confusion and the joy of immeasurable
abundance for which life can never again compensate." And
still later, when Herr von Andergast seeks out the rector to
have a talk with him about Etzel, we are given another
glimpse of the profound disturbances which are taking place
in the boy's soul. "It always seems as if Etzel walked about
absent-mindedly in the normal channels and were seizing
every opportunity that offered to dodge around the corner in
order to execute some secret understanding of his own. When
he reappears he looks as if he had stolen something and were
quickly and slyly secreting his booty. And indeed it is all
stealing, the experiences which he seeks and which cannot
be examined, the words and thoughts which he is accumu-
lating, the pictures with which he is storing his insatiable
fantasy. Everywhere he finds accomplices, every door opens
into the world and all new knowledge of the world sullies

this untarnished soul." "That boy has a restless spirit," the rector remarks. "Really he will only believe what can be proven as clearly as daylight. . . Even God Himself would not have an easy time with him."

Here are the beginnings then of a saint or a devil. Clearly Etzel is full of character. One is tempted to say of such a restless spirit that he has the makings of an artist. And even though God Himself might have a difficult time with him, is it not precisely such souls whom God delights to win over? Is it not true that it is only from the restless, tormented spirits that we may expect great things? In the second volume, when we observe the healing influence of Dr. Kerkhoven at work on the boy, we are led to entertain great hopes. But these, alas, are soon dispelled. Even such an extraordinary healer as Kerkhoven is powerless here. If there had been no Marie perhaps Kerkhoven might have made headway. But Marie is precisely the embodiment of a temptation which Etzel is unable to fight against. Marie, wilting for lack of proper affection, replaces that lost fountain of love which Etzel longed for in the mother. Marie becomes affection itself for him. And he, no longer mindful now of "duty," allows himself to drown in the ocean of her affection.

The picture we get in this volume of Etzel's life after drifting from the paternal home, is like an intimate study of a cross section of civilized society. *What a Germany!* one mutters to himself. What a viper's nest! Nothing but corruption, doubt, disillusiomnent, crime. Here we see the soil out of which the future schizophrenic type, the Steppenwolfs* of tomorrow, will spring. *What a Germany!* Ah, but is it Germany alone we are dealing with here? What about France? What about Italy, Spain, Hungary, Poland, Roumania? What about England? What about our own United States of America? It is necessary to redescribe these festering charnel

---

*See Herman Hesse's Steppenwolf, a novel.

houses? Think of the youth Céline describes in *Mort à Crédit*. Could a cannibal lead a more ugly, hopeless life than the youthful Ferdinand in that garden of culture, France? For a picture of perversion and hypocrisy, of monstrous stupidity and insensitiveness, turn to Cyril Connolly's *Enemies of Promise*. What man, unless he were made of iron, could survive that special kind of training which goes by the name of education in the English schools? I think immediately of another Englishman, describing another kind of life, equally bitter, futile and contemptible, but typical of our civilized society: George Orwell's *Down and Out in Paris and London*. And from that to Arthur Koestler is but a step. In Koestler's works all Europe is arraigned and found guilty. Everywhere we encounter men whose hands are steeped in blood. Everywhere the man hunt. Everywhere accuser and accused. Not injustice, but intolerance, is the theme which pervades all Koestler's books. With it goes a complete lack of human dignity and the betrayal of all human standards. The heroes lie in the mud and are trampled on: *Scum of the Earth*. Objects of pity or contempt. Ignored, left to wither, to rot. And in Russia, where the great social experiment has been going on for some twenty years or more now, what do we find there? Is this the last refuge of hope for the white man in Europe? Read Koestler's *Darkness at Noon*. This trial, reminiscent of other celebrated trials in European history, makes us sick to the guts. Is it exaggerated? Nothing could be exaggerated nowadays. No villainy, no crime, nothing however vile, ignoble or degrading is beneath the present day members of our civilized world. The Inquisition is here again; now it burns in Germany, now in Russia, now in Italy, now in Spain, now in France. Kafka's long nightmares were but a preparation for the actual horrors we were to experience even to a greater degree. In India practically every able and intelligent leader is in prison or in exile. In Greece, in Belgium, in

Poland, the people have been betrayed by the very ones who were to deliver them from their oppressors. No wonder that in England we have a man like Alex Comfort shouting at the top of his voice (and no one as yet has clamped down on him) that "*society* is the enemy," *this* society, this so-called *civilized* society. Years before the present outbreak, the man who is now condemned as a "collaborationist," the man who is for this generation what Romain Rolland was to the last, the man of truth and worshipper of the good and beautiful, Jean Giono, raised his voice in like manner. In *Refus D' Obéissance* we have the poignant rebellion of a man of spirit who realized that the sacrifice which was made in the last war was in vain. Where Comfort now uses the word Society, Giono uses The Capitalist State. Today we see that it is not only the Capitalist State which is guilty, but every form of government now practised throughout the civilized world. Hence, when reading Giono, one ought to substitute Society.

Here is how Giono begins his heart-rending recital:

"I cannot forget the War. I wish I could. Sometimes several days go by without my thinking of it, then suddenly I see it once more, I feel it, I hear it, I suffer it anew. And I am afraid . . .

"I am not ashamed of myself. In 1913 I refused to join the military preparations which gathered all my comrades. In 1915 I departed for the front without believing in *la patrie*. I was wrong. Not in not believing, but in going. . .

"I know I never killed anybody. I went through all the attacks without a gun, or rather with a gun that was useless. (All the survivors of the War know how easy it was, with a little earth and piss, to turn a Lebel rifle into a stick.)

"I am not ashamed, but to consider well what I have done, it was a cowardly act to have gone to war, I had the air of accepting. I did not have the courage to say: 'I will not leave for the attack.' I did not have the courage to desert. I have only one excuse: it is that I was young. I am not a coward. I was duped by my immaturity and I was equally duped by those who knew that I was immature. . . .

"*War is not a catastrophe . . . it is a means of government.* The Capitalist State does not recognize the men who seek what we call happiness, the men whose nature is to be what they are, the men of flesh and bone—it only knows them as material for producing capital. To produce capital, it has, at certain times, need of war . . .

"In the Capitalist State those who enjoy, enjoy only blood and gold. What it causes to be said by its laws, its professors, its accredited writers, is that there is *the duty of sacrificing one's self. It is necessary that you, I and the others, we sacri-*fice ourselves. To whom?

"The Capitalist State politely hides from us the road to the slaughterhouse: you sacrifice yourselves for your country (already they dare not say that any more), but after all, *for your neighbor, for your children, for future generations.* And so forth, from generation to generation. Who then eats the fruits of this sacrifice in the end?

"I speak objectively. Here is an organism which is functioning. It is called Capitalist State, as it might be called dog, cat, or caterpillar. It is there, spread on my table, belly open. I see its organism functioning. In this organism, if I take away war, I disorganize it so violently that I render it incapable of life—just as if I took away the heart of the dog, as if I dissected the motor centre of the caterpillar.

"Let us continue to be objective. Of what use is my sacrifice? None! *(I hear! do not shout so loudly in the shadows. Do not show your horrid mouths, you victims of the factory. Don't speak, you who say your workshop is closed and that there is no bread in the house. Do not howl against the gate of that chateau where there is dancing. I hear!)* My sacrifice serves nothing, except to prolong the existence of the Capitalist State.

"This Capitalist State, does it merit my sacrifice? Is it kind, patient, amiable, human, honest? Is it seeking happiness for all? Is it carried by its sidereal movement towards goodness and beauty, and does it carry war within itself only as the earth carries its central hearth? I do not ask these questions to answer them for myself. *I ask them so that everyone will answer them for himself.*"

That is the tone and spirit of Giono, as polemist and propagandist. That is the type of man who nowadays is branded as a traitor. There is another Giono, an even greater one, who wrote *Le Chant du Monde* and *Que Ma Joie Demeure*. This is the Giono who is in love with life, who seeks out "the beauties of earth," who revels in all nature's creations from highest to lowest, the man who loves children, the man of the soil, the man who was an inspiration to all who came in contact with him. And such a man is now a traitor? I refuse to believe it. I say there is something wrong with a society which, because it quarrels with a man's views, can condemn him as an arch-enemy. Giono is not a traitor. Society is the traitor. Society is a traitor to its fine principles, its empty principles. Society is constantly looking for victims—and finds them among the glorious in spirit.

But that is Society for you. A guilty society in the grip of fear. Always smelling and sniffing, always fearful of invasion, always pointing an accusing finger. Every man stands guilty. Every man is loaded with guilt—from birth. If ever there was a guilty age, this is it. Guilt and hysteria. And at the bottom of it all, like an evil dragon, lies Fear.

To come back to *The Maurizius Case* . . . Observe, please, how all the characters are riddled with guilt. Even Maurizius, the innocent one. Especially Maurizius, let us say. Is it not he who says: "Man is cut off from man by guilt?" Each one, Elli, the wife, Anna Jahn, her sister, old man Maurizius, Baron von Andergast, Waremme-Warshauer—all squirm with guilt.

The innocent one! Let us concentrate on him for a moment, on the peculiar nature of his plight, as viewed by the law, by society itself. Maurizius has pregnant words to deliver on this subject. Let us hear what he says when that model of justice, Herr von Andergast, visits him in his cell and repeats what men of law everywhere in the civilized world so frequently, tritely, and unthinkingly reiterate.

Herr von Andergast has just said: "Everyone is regarded as innocent so long as his guilt has not been indisputably established."

And here is what Maurizius answers: "It is written thus. Can't be denied. A good many things are written. But will you assert that it is carried out? Where? When? To whom? On whom? . . . As I have said, I am not referring to my personal circumstances . . . I have not only had my own experience, I have had a thousand. I have heard of a thousand judges, I have seen a thousand before me and I have been able to observe the work of a thousand, and it is always the same thing. From the first he is the enemy. For him the deed has been done, he takes the human being at his lowest. The accuser is his god, the accused his victim, punishment his goal. If one has gotten to the point of appearing before a judge, one is done for . . . Judge! That formerly had a high meaning. The highest in human society. I have known people who have told me that at every trial they have the same horrible feeling in their testicles that one has if one suddenly stands over a deep abyss. Every cross-examination depends upon the employment of tactical advantages which one mostly secures just as dishonestly as the subterfuges of a victim at bay . . . How can one obtain the protection which your law ·demands? The law is only a pretext for the cruel organizations created in its name, and how can one be expected to bow down before a judge who makes of a guilty human being a maltreated animal? . . . It all comes to the fact that those who live in heaven have no conception of hell, even if one tells them about it for days. There all fantasy fails. Only he can undestand who is in it."

And then, after further words from von Andergast of the imperfection of human institutions and the impracticability of destroying the whole structure, Maurizius is goaded into delivering word for word fragments from the condemnatory speech made by Andergast himself. It is the portrait of a criminal made by the criminal himself. Not the criminal, Maurizius, but the criminal, von Andergast. Here is how von Andergast reflects to himself on the words he delivered eighteen years ago:

"The repetition, accurate almost to a word, of a speech made almost half a generation ago, filled him with astonishment; but the curious thing was that nothing about it seemed familiar, or known to him, the author of it, although he could judge with a fair degree of certainty that Maurizius had not altered or distorted it; it was rather that it seemed to him like something strange, something unpleasant and distasteful, exaggerated, full of phrases and rhetoric and forced contrasts. As he gazed down upon the cowering convict, his dislike of his own oratory, which he had just heard out of this man's mouth, grew into physical disgust, so that he had finally to struggle against the inclination to vomit; he had to grit his teeth convulsively. It was as if his words crawled along the wall like worms, slimy, colorless, hateful, ugly. If all achievement was so fleeting, so temporary, so questionable, how could one bear to be tested? If a truth for which one had once been willing to vouch before God and man could after a time become a piece of buffoonery, how did matters stand with 'truth' in general? Or was it only that something in him had decayed, that the framework of his ego had broken down?"

And now it is Maurizius talking again, telling of his romantic youth. He has just finished telling Andergast about the pure love he felt for a prostitute at the age of sixteen, and of the tragic dénouement of that episode in his life. "Perhaps as a matter of fact one never recovers from such a thing," he says. In those years, as he puts it, everything egotistical was sporadic and whoever did not decidedly break with his surroundings and tradition was gradually swamped and disposed of, and had to get on as best he could with his black moods. As he says, one could be "romantic" and have very little conscience.

And then follows this most significant speech:

"I still remember that at nineteen I came home from a performance of Tristan, a happy, new-born person, and then I stole twenty marks from my father's bureau drawer. Both were compatible. Always both were compatible. To swear to a girl a sacred oath that one would marry her and shortly afterwards leave her contemptibly to her fate, and in an exalted mood to read and assimilate the life and works of Buddha. To do a poor tailor out of his earnings and to stand enthralled before a Raphael Madonna. One could be tremendously moved at the theatre over Hauptmann's *Weavers* and read with satisfaction that the strikers in the Ruhr were being fired upon. Both. Always the two were possible . . . There you have another portrait. A self-portrait. Do you think it is more flattering than yours? Its only redeeming feature is in its admitting two possibilities each time. Yours is cruelty implacable because it admits only one."

It is in Waremme-Warschauer, however, that duality really flowers. "Everything that was said about him was just as correct as the exact opposite would have been." Master of a dozen languages, a poet, philosopher, philologist and politician, he is also a gambler, a Don Juan, a pervert, a perjurer and renegade. In him the chancre which is at the very heart of society flowers luxuriantly. As the most gifted, the most cultured, figure in the book, he is a veritable flower of evil. In one of those interminable monologues which he holds in Etzel's presence, he makes mention once of an Oriental saying which, it seems to me, is particularly applicable to himself. "If a man is separated from his soul and the yearning of his soul, he does not remain standing in the road, but hastens his wanderings." Looking back upon his youth, Waremme says to Etzel: "I could take people by storm, I could kindle their enthusiasm endlessly, I could . . . What could I not do? . . . I could give them their own souls over again . . To me my communication was my other nature, my real nature like the beat of my pulse: where I could communicate myself I already identified myself; it was the most sublime form of love towards men and women, a tireless siege to drive the others out of themselves, to free them from all barriers and reserves. I myself had none, neither barriers nor reserves, that was just it. . ."

In the course of one of these monologues a contrasting picture is made between Europe and America. Waremme had spent something like twelve years in some of our great American cities, including Chicago. He had tried to break with Europe. But, as he so aptly puts it, "to turn one's back upon Europe does not yet mean to be able to live without it." Only after renouncing it could a person of his sort, he confesses, begin to understand what Europe actually meant. "Europe was not merely the sum total of the ties of his own individual existence, friendship and love, hatred and unhappiness, success and disappointment; it was, venerable and intangible, the existence of a unity of two thousand years, Pericles and Nostradamus, Theodoric and Voltaire, Ovid and Erasmus, Archimedes and Gauss, Calderon and Durer, Phidias and Mozart, Petrarch and Napoleon, Galileo and Nietzsche, an immeasurable army of geniuses and an equally immeasurable army of demons. All this light driven into darkness and shining forth from it again, a sordid morass producing a golden vessel, the catastrophes and inspirations, the revolutions and periods of darkness, the moralities and the fashions, all that great common stream with its chains, its stages, and its pinnacles, making up one spirit. That was Europe, that was his Europe."

And so Waremme departs for America, a sort of Columbus the Second, to proclaim the spirit of Europe. And what happens? "After a few weeks," he relates, "I was entirely destitute. That did not worry me much. No one can starve over there. The whole country is, so to speak, a huge scheme of insurance against starvation. The public charities are so gigantic that beggars are almost as scarce as kings. And they have democracy. *What lies between living and not starving is another matter.** Conceive of a tremendous hospital, furnished with every modern comfort, filled with the incurable sick, not one of whom ever dies, and you will have what lies "between." *Deaths would damage the reputation of the establishment. . ."**

It is all so tremendous, so unbearably immense, the individual scarcely has any name any longer, the separate thing nothing, nothing to differentiate it. Numbered streets, why not numbered people, perhaps numbered according to the dollars they earn with the blood of cattle, with the soul of the world?" Then Halsted Street, the longest street in the world—*the new road to Golgotha.* And then the Negro,

*Italics mine

He goes on to speak of his inability to communicate anything of the spirit to those Americans he came in contact
with. "No," he muses, "they do not love the spirit; they
loved the thing, the object, they loved performance, eulogy,
a fact, but spirit is to them mysterious beyond all measure.
They have something in its place, the smile. I had to learn
to smile." And so he wanders from one city to another. "Jack
tosses you to John, John to Bill, and when Bill finds out that
you are no longer any good, he leaves you on the junk-heap
—all in quite friendly fashion, of course. Keep smiling!"

And then to Chicago. . . the thirty thousand canaries
which have just been unpacked, singing out of thirty thous-
and tiny throats. . . drowning out the noise of cranes and
motors, the screams of locomotives and people. He stands
there, not knowing whether to laugh or to cry. "It is so mad,
so holy and so fairylike." Then the stockyards. . . "where the
sweetish smell of blood rises from the tremendous halls and
warehouses, a constant cloud of blood hangs over the whole
city: the people's clothes smell of blood, their beds, their
churches, their rooms, their food, their wines, their kisses.
Joshua Cooper. And Joshua covered with blood and running
the gauntlet. Waremme speaks now with unrestrained passion. "Beasts! Why, every beast has the soul of a Quaker
compared to theirs . . . Acherontic figures, the two-legged
beasts of the suburbs. We haven't that kind in this country;
the most depraved here reminds one still that a mother has
borne him. . ."

Finally in this long tirade there comes a ray of light. It
comes from the "beaming birthday face" of Hamilton La
Due. In the person of La Due, Waremme begins to perceive
the potential American, the true democrat of which Whitman sang. "I saw a human being who, for all his insignificant
exterior, represented a unity, the crystal formed from the
raw material. There were probably countless persons like

him, and the more I looked into this tremendous complex the more I became convinced that he actually was only one of countless men like himself whom I had accidentally found. This shook my European pride profoundly. . ." He goes on to say of La Due that he had no message, was no evangelist, that he had simple child-like friendliness, nothing else. "He probably did not think about matters at all. He accepted everything as it was, the frightful and pleasant. . ." And then, in a spate of eloquence, Waremme summarizes the meaning of this person La Due. "In that tremendous nation, with its tremendous cities, tremendous mountains and torrents and prairies, its tremendous riches and tremendous poverty, its tremendous factories and tremendous fear of anarchy and revolution, there in the midst of all that we find harmless little La Due. . . how shall I put it, as a new kind of human being. I could not cease wondering. Through him I learned to understand that the whole is still an unleavened mass. . ."

It's rather curious that the man who is represented as the Devil incarnate should be able to recognize the exemplary character of a figure like Hamilton La Due. Is it because he is a thoroughly inconspicuous figure, this La Due, a simple man with no pretensions of any kind, a man unconscious of his own goodness? For Etzel too there is one man whom he reveres and whom finally he goes to visit: Mechior Ghisels, the writer. Indeed, this Ghisels has become in Etzel's mind almost a god. But this god, upon closer contact, turns out to be all too human. He is a god who has exhausted himself through sacrifice. When Etzel finds him he is lying prostrate on the couch, a man so used up that he is unable to make fitting answer to the burning question—"What then is justice if I do not see it through, I, myself, I, Etzel Andergast?" And Ghisels, looking for all the world like a man crucified, can only answer: "I have nothing to reply to that except: Forgive me, I am but a feeble man." As Etzel takes leave of

Ghisels he recalls a beautiful phrase which once had meant so much to him, and then, says the author, Etzel understood in his heart that "the ten thousand angels upon the rose-leaf were a metaphor, a poem, a mysterious and beautiful symbol, nothing further, oh, nothing more than that."

There are aspects of this interview which I would like to dwell on a little more. In the first place Ghisels seems to be the mouthpiece for the author himself. There are resemblances between the lives of the two men which cannot be ignored. Wassermann too was overburdened by the insatiable demands of his readers. People believed him to be something more than a writer; his books contained a promise which the words of political and social theorizers lacked. In this conversation with Etzel, Wassermann uses Ghisels to make his own prophetic picture of European society and the crisis which it faced. It is as though he had the boy Etzel, his own tormented creation, walk out of the pages of the book and search him out in his own study. As thought Etzel stood before him, pounding upon his own desk, and shouting: "I demand an answer! You placed me in this impossible situation, now help me to extricate myself!" It is as if Wassermann were dissatisfied with his own verbal skill, his own inventiveness, as if he were tired of these perpetual human problems which can never be answered directly through art; as if he were challenging himself to a last supreme effort, the god-like effort of a man risen above all personal considerations, who knows that on the human level there is no solution to these problems. With *The Marizius Case* Wassermann is approaching the end of his own life. He seems to have mustered all his forces for this final work. In the last volume of the trilogy his own appearance is unmistakable. As Herzog, the broken-down novelist, he too seeks out a figure whom he has long revered. Dr. Kerkhoven is an exalted being; he is superior to the author himself. It is like the Creator confront-

ing his own creation and being vanquished, *justly* vanquished. Kerkhoven is a symbol of the healer. How significant that
the artist should have elevated to the highest position the
type of which the world stands most in need at this moment!
If it appears that Ghisels failed Etzel at the crucial moment,
we must remember that he is being judged by a sixteen year
old boy whose experience of life does not permit him to
understand the limitations of the artist. We must also remember, it seems to me, that Wassermann was probably
condemning himself, and through himself all artists of our
time. Looking at Ghisels thus, how pregnant then are the
author's words: "This is the meaning which he [Etzel] thinks
he has discovered in the writings: *That one must go a step
further.*" This phrase, as one burrows deeper into the trilogy,
becomes haunting and obsessive. It is this phrase which
describes the essential quality of that monumental figure,
Kerkhoven. Kerkhoven is always starting anew, always daring to break the bounds—*his own bounds.*

Perhaps now we can look back upon Ghisel's words with
greater clarity. Here is how he speaks to Etzel: "What brings
you to me is nothing new to me—unfortunately. It is a crisis
which has gone beyond making harmless circles in a pool.
A few years ago one could still console oneself with the
opinion that it was this or that isolated case, one could ad-
just oneself to that—one can get used to the isolated in-
stances—but today we are threatened with the collapse of
the whole structure which we have been building for two
thousand years. There is an ingrained sick desire to break
things down, in the most sensitive human beings. If this
cannot be stopped—and I fear it is already too late—it must
lead within the next fifty years to a frightful collapse, far
worse than any wars or revolutions up to the present. Curious, the disturbance often proceeds from those who live in
the delusion that they are called upon to safeguard what are

termed our most sacred possessions."

Etzel listens attentively, but like a boxer waiting for an opening. It is justice he wants to hear about. "Justice, it seems to me, is the beating heart of the world. Is that so, or is it not?" he asks. And then Ghisels makes answer.

"It is so, dear friend. Justice and love were originally sisters. In our civilization they are no longer even distant relatives. One may give many explanations without explaining anything. We no longer have a people, a people constituting the body politic; that which we call democracy is founded upon an amorphous mass and cannot dispose itself and elevate itself intelligently and strangles all ideality. Perhaps we need a Caesar. But where shall he come from? And we must fear the chaos that would produce him. What the best people do in the best case is to provide a commentary for an earthquake. . ."

He continues in a moment. "I should only like to tell you one thing. Think about it a little; perhaps it will help you on a step, for we can only move forward very, very slowly, and step by step. . . It is not a means of salvation, not a tremendous truth which I have in mind, but perhaps, as I have said, it is a hint, a useful suggestion. . . What I mean is this: good and evil are not determined by the intercourse of people with one another, but entirely by a man's relations with himself. Do you understand?"

Etzel nods. He understands, yes, quite clearly. *But*—Well, in a sense he doesn't want to understand. There is something bothering him, something he will never understand. If some one is imprisoned unjustly, what then? What is he to do in such a case? Is he to forget about the person? Is he to leave the man in torment? Is he to say to himself, how does that concern me? How does one's relation to himself help him in such a case? And then he fires at Ghisels the question which the latter cannot answer. In a few moments completely disillusioned, he takes leave of the man he once worshipped. He must carry on—it's war. He must see that justice is established, no matter what happens.

And now let us return to the most enigmatic figure in the book: Anna Jahn, the murderess. Everything revolves about Anna Jahn. Truly everything. She is the fulcrum on which the whole drama rests. She is like motionless glass. All the horrible events which weave themselves into an inextricable web, which roll up finally like so many cocoons and suffocate all concerned, seem to have their origin in the mere fact of Anna Jahn's existence. She is like a Borgia in reverse. She seems to do nothing, unless it be to inspire misfortune. She is all seeming, that is it. She mirrors the desires, the hopes, the dreams and illusions of every one with whom she comes in contact. She is evil—because she has made herself powerless to act.

What is her crime, precisely? Stupidity. When you think of it, nothing worse could be said about such a character than this, that she was abysmally stupid. The scene between her and Maurizius when the latter, released from prison, ferrets her out is almost too terrible to read. "Time," says Wassermann, "which either covers over generously, or exposes cruelly, has a sovereign manner of finally revealing what, from lack of a true measure and proportion, appears to the human eye a hopeless intricacy of mysterious depths. The original simplicity of fate, when the vague clouds of the fleeting moment have been dissipated. Even the word-magic of a Waremme cannot alter this. Those who imagine that they justify themselves before God or elucidate their confused meanderings by twisting the simplicity of the world into a magnificent mystery, are the real damned, for they cannot be saved from themselves."

Yet, despite Wassermann's sovereign dismissal of her, we must turn for a last picture of her to Waremme. Waremme knows her down to the roots, knows her even better than Wassermann, if one may say such an absurd thing. He knows her pitilessly, like the surgeon's scalpel. And why shouldn't he? Has she not lived in him like a festering wound?

It is on the night when Etzel finally extorts from Waremme the confession he has been waiting for so long that we get this fluoroscopic portrait of Anna Jahn. And with it the clue to the whole tragedy. We understand at last why Maurizius acted as he did, why he was bound as if by fate.

"I shall now say something which no one in the world except you and I know," Waremme begins. "It may seem at first something very usual, but in view of the person in question, it is very unusual. It is that which made me the final arbiter. When I understood the situation, I felt as if a giant had seized me and broken my back. Namely, she loved the man (Maurizius), that was it. She loved him so, with such a furious passion, that her mind became clouded and she became incurably ill. This was the profoundest thing to her, this love; it was the leap into Orcus. And he, he did not know it. He didn't even have a notion of it. He for his part merely loved her, the unfortunate man, but he begged and wooed her and whined, whereas she, she had already taken the plunge. That he did not know this—this she could not forgive. That she loved him so endlessly—she never forgave either him or herself for it. For that he had to suffer punishment. He must no longer be in the world. That she had shot her sister for his sake must never, under any circumstances, build a bridge from him to her. She had made this an iron law for herself and she immured herself in it. She created his death, she created his expiration, she was his most cruel persecutor, and in order to bear his life and his punishment with him, she transformed herself into a souless fury. At the same time she had a bourgeois pride and a bourgeois cowardice along with it, which one will scarcely find again combined to such a degree in one person. . . No, Mohl (Etzel), you cannot understand that character, and I must say, Heaven forbid that you should. A savage pagan and a silly bigot, full of arrogance and a passion for self-destruction; chaste as an altarpiece and flaming with a mystic dark sensuality like a primeval forest; strict, but hungering for tenderness; surrounding herself with insurmountable barriers, hating anyone who attempted to break them down, hating him who respected them—and all this, above all, under an evil star. There are many people who live under an evil star. They lack light. They desire their dark fate and they pursue it for so long and challenge it until it comes forth and tramples upon them. That was how it was with her. . ."

In his little cell Maurizius of course had reflected upon the nature of this woman endlessly, and he too has made terrible judgment upon her. To know anything about her one would have to cut open her breast and examine her heart, he thinks to himself. There is no real kernel to her nature. "She is destructive, banefully solitary and selfcentered, limited in herself and to her own fate." Speaking aloud to himself, in von Andergast's presence, he sums up the relationship in one word: Narcissism. "Vessels to which we give the content, perhaps even the soul, certainly their motion and destination. Perhaps they only become our victims because they are so narcissistically bound up in themselves. And what is narcissim? It is something which has no body and they make us responsible, make us pay to the day of judgment for wanting to embrace something which has no body, a mere counterfeit of a human. . ."

Sometimes, in thinking of Anna Jahn, for in my mind she

is alive and her roots are everywhere, in all our thoughts, all our actions. . . sometimes, I say, I get to comparing her with women I have known who resemble her, all of them mysterious figures, extraordinarily beautiful, seductively sorrowful or melancholy, and all of them distinctly angelic. In each case they move as in a web, spinning the fates of those about them with each step they make, their lives inextricably bound up with other lives, but to such a degree that if one were to attempt to separate them with the shears one would find himself cutting into a sponge-like fungus—or into one of those balls made of rubber bands which children make in order to see them bounce above the roof-tops. If one so much as dares to open a door into the lives of such persons one is immediately sucked in as if by a vacuum. They are like flowers that swallow you whole and digest you during the night. With all these angelic vampires I have found one curious fact which repeats itself—they manage to get violated in early youth. The Filipovna woman (in Dostoievski) is a classic example. But even in life they are classic, all classic examples. One never wholly accepts them as life-like: they come down to us from the pages of books, from the dreams of saints and madmen. What tender hearts they seem to have! until one sounds the depth of their cruelty, which is abysmal. Knives and revolvers flourish in their presence, but one does not even wonder at the incongruity of these appurtenances, so natural does it seem that these seraphic beings assist at every performance of crime. Truly, their presence among us is mysterious, for they are neither of this earth nor of the under-world. In the garden of feminine diversity they are like black camellias. They are the flowers in which angels disguise themselves when they have forgotten their origin. Their lost innocence operates as a magnet which permits the organism to embrace every contradiction and irradiate confusion. The earth turns upon its axis once a day, but these lost angels refuse not only to revolve but to die. From life they pass quickly into legend and from legend back into life again. Their death is only a *Scheintot*.

When in my imagination I direct the film of *The Maurizius Case* I see Anna Jahn appearing in every scene. I cannot imagine any of the characters existing except in and through her. If I see her naked, she is then like one of those medieval French virgins who illuminate the pages of rare books. If I see her clothed, it is always in the velvety seduction of her own white skin. Whenever she appears flowers spring up, flowers heavy with dew and of overpowering fragrance; they spring up in her wake, like the phosphorescent fireworks created by a swift ocean greyhound. Perpetually there hovers about her lips a smile. But it is a smile of such infinite sadness that one does not recognize it; it is like a pale crescent moon of a night when the stars are intoxicatingly brilliant. From this body in which so much sorrow and splendour are anchored there proceeds a constant emanation of wrath-like figures, all Anna Jahns, but all varying in brillance and gravity, as if she were spewing forth an infinite calculus of her own atomic weight. This lends to every meeting an atmosphere of ultra lucidity. (Blake's Vegetable Eye.) The corporeal and the spiritual intermingle, but diaphanously. Everything takes place in the "airs," the cue being given from the netherworld. On the plane of narcissism, where she is stuck like an abandoned lighthouse, the drama makes no sense whatever. She is simply an heraldic field in which symbolism wins the day. Nothing stirs in her soul, for she is of glass through and through, and motionless. But in the emanations all the powers and principalities mirror their conflicts as in a whirlpool. And from wraith to wraith, caught as they are in the myriad filaments of a giant cocoon, tremors pass convulsive as the shudders of *an incinerated octopus.*

Here I must leave Anna Jahn for the time being. May her soul rest in peace. It is another day and my mind is no longer working in cinematopgraphic images. "Augustine says God must exist because he has come upon Him in the vast palaces of his memory." I read this in one of Wallace Fowlie's books recently. The words haunt me, especially that phrase "in the vast palaces of his memory."

The Maurizius Case is full of vast palaces of memory. But somehow God is absent. Every character in the book, it seems, certainly all the principal ones, are exuding their memories of sorrow and despair. By the time one drops the book one has the impression of having inhabited a charnel house. The memories have turned to dead bone and the bones are full of worms. Maurizius is memory incarnate. In him every one lives and dies again and again. Not only individuals but races, civilizations. Every night he grows a new forest of memories. Every night? Every minute of the day, for the minutes are divided into seconds and the seconds are light years apart. As for Waremme, in him whole cultures are recapitulated, digested, and thrown to the dogs. In him we live through the golden epochs of the past. He is there like a filtered through him, even the knowledge of God. He is the voice of nostalgia. He is even lonelier than the prisoner Maurizius. Nothing can assuage his misery: he is the very spirit of a dying age. In him the doom of the cultural world resounds like the lost voice of the dinosaur. He lives in the "phenomenology of mind."

All are anguished souls—Andergast, Elli the wife, Anna Jahn, Etzel's mother, old man Maurizius, all of them. What a Germany! What a world! And yet it is a world full of riches, as Waremme is constantly revealing to us. It is not the Wasteland of Eliot's morbid imagination. Nor is it the Germany of this precise chronological moment when, according to newspaper reports, 20,000,000 souls are running about like cockroaches, not knowing how or where to escape the on-coming bombs. In this Germany there are still beautiful tableaux: one feels culture everywhere, even inside the prison walls. People converse in a language which is exhilarating and often lofty. Despite the bourgeois frame in which the drama takes place there is a warm, human glow pervading everything. Spirit is there, even if defiled. It is not a desert. It is not a vacuum. Much of all this we owe to Wassermann, but most we owe to Europe itself. Even the failure to solve the problem we owe to Europe, to that rounded view of things which recognizes that tragedy is of the very essence of the world.

Only this morning I was glancing at some old postcards from Europe. What a terrible nostalgia I felt! Many of these street corners no longer exist; many of the cathedrals have been blown to smithereens. But they will be rebuilt. Europe will always have a different look from our world. Older, scarred, riddled with memories. A more human look, despite the ceaseless strife and carnage which has filled its history. We need this world, even if there isn't a single Hamilton La Due with "beaming birthday face" in it. We need men who despair as well as men who hope. But above all, we need the riches of Europe. America is an impoverished land: it has everything and nothing. True, men like La Due exist here, but not like blades of grass. And if I were asked my honest opinion, if I were asked in which I would choose to live, the world of La Due or the world of Waremme, I would choose the latter. Even if Waremme be the Devil incarnate, one can have conversation with such a fellow, one is at home with him. Are there not plenty of devils and demons on the façades of the great cathedrals? One does not turn away from the great portals of a cathedral because the Devil too is rep-resented. In La Due's world I see no symbolic edifices of any kind. I recognize the warm heart, the sound instincts, the desire to serve, and I give it full due. But it takes more than these to build a world.

The Maurizius, like the Dreyfus Case, the Tom Mooney Case, the Sacco Vanzetti Case, the Bridges Case—what a dossier of cases one could compile!—fills one with sadness and despair not because there has been a miscarriage of justice but because society itself is revealed as a vast web in which all its members, good and bad, are pinioned and squirm helplessly. All intelligent members of society know that the legal and moral codes of their respective lands are inadequate, but what they do not know, until we have a celebrated "case", is that nothing can be done, that everyone's hands are tied. Only when a flaming injustice is being perpetrated do we realize how empty the world culture is. Suddenly the whole edifice is seen to be rotten—the worms become visible. The historical tide carries us along: we nod or groan or close our eyes. One case succeeds another, and then finally there is a holocaust. The edifice crumbles, totters, crashes about our ears. Another chapter is added to our ignominious history. But man survives everything, even the worms.

Perhaps the most terrible things that can be said about civilized man is that his enlightenment in no way aids him to ameliorate conditions. In every grave conflict we see that there are forces at work which are beyond his control. He can elect to espouse the good, but that does not signify that he can accomplish the good. The very fervour with which he sacrifices himself is often suspect. Etzel Andergast, as we have pointed out before, is an example of the type which agitates for the good and the right for wrong motives. He symbolizes, an extent, the tragic dilemma of society as a whole which finds its nemesis in the unconscious. Of what use the noble, exalted ideals inculcated by our culture if we are to be continually betrayed by our ineradicable passion? To beseech us to stop and tackle our problems from another angle, as Klakusch urges, is impossible. We and our problems are one creation. Each age has its own peculiar problems, just as each type of individual has his own. The better the man the greater his problems. And so with a people, so with an epoch. It is our peculiar plight, in this age, to be conscious of solutions which we know are possible for us to make. Solutions, I say, and not adjustments. The all-pervading neurosis in which the members of our civilized society are gripped means just that. That is why, I imagine, Wassermann moved on from the impasse of the Maurizius Case to the more involved and even more desperate impasse of Doctor Kerhhoven, the chief figure in the second book of the trilogy. But what does Kerkhoven find? Exactly what all our healers today are up against—the fact that he cannot cope with the multitude of sick people who besiege him. Psycho-analysis is no solution, any more than the second coming of Christ would be. To cure the sick conscience of the world a totally new outlook on life is necessary. Not a Saviour. Each man will have to save himself, now if never before. Because now we know that no other solution is possible. We have tried them all, again and again. That is the lesson of history—the futility of all other attempts. That is the meaning of the rat-trap which is called the cyclical interpretation of history. No matter if some perceive within the cycle repetitions an upward or a downward spiralling. . . the cycle must be broken. There must be egress or man as we know him will revert to some sub-human level. That is the issue. It will not be decided overnight, by war or revolution, nor by a religious revival. It will take centuries of struggle. And man has the endurance for it, especially as he becomes more and more aware of the nature of that struggle. In a sense, this is an Apocalyptic struggle. Man is now facing two ways—backwards and forwards. He has a choice, as he never had before.

He has forged a new conscience and that means that he must go forward to a new level of consciousness or face annihilation. This is not a thought reserved only for metaphysicians and analysts. It is in the heart of every man today, and it goads and torments him, making him the sick and the helpless creature which he is.

I am not talking of a millenium to come. There will be perpetual conflict, perpetual war. But these problems which have sickened us to death will soon be non-existent. We will have moved on to another plane, able to cope with greater, nobler problems. Wars will not cease. This particular form of suffering which goes by the name of war will still be indispensable, if only for the reason that as men move towards a higher level of consciousness the ability to dispense with the purely physical means of expression becomes more critical, more in question. There is a tremendous stretch of darkness to be traversed and it is a darkness filled with rivers of blood. What the four centuries of plague and pestilence were for Europe, wars and revolutions will be for the future of the entire world. But these cataclysms will take on a different character as we move through them. One has only to think of the various stages of initiation, of their increasingly terrifying quality, to understand what is meant here. Every birth of consciousness demands an agony supreme and heretofore unequalled. And we are, without a doubt, at the threshhold of a new vision of things. However terrifying the prospect, there is this to be said for it—the birth of a new age exalts men's courage. The despair and disgust with which men have been going to war these last centuries will give way as they begin to perceive the light of a new day.

FINIS

MOTHER, CHINA, AND THE WORLD BEYOND

HENRY MILLER

1977

PREFATORY NOTE

This text was inspired by a dream in which I died and found myself in Devachan (limbo) where I ran into my mother whom I hated all my life.

MOTHER

I didn't quite realize I had died—I seemed so alive—until I saw my mother approaching. Then it struck me that I too must be what we call dead. I hadn't had time to take note of my surroundings; everything seemed so natural even if different.

What immediately struck me was the radiant expression on my mother's face. (That was indeed something new to me.) She looked younger than I had ever known her, even when a boy. She was almost gay.

"O Henry," she exclaimed, as we drew close, "you don't know how glad I am to see you. I waited for you such a long time. What ever kept you on Earth so long?"

A spate of words rushed to my lips but all I could utter was "Mother, dear Mother." Besides, there seemed no necessity for words. I was alive still, but in a new sense. I had a different intelligence, a whole new set of emotions. Above all, I was at peace—in a state of bliss, rather.

"Where are we?" I finally managed to say.

My mother shrugged her shoulders smilingly. "I don't know," she replied. Nobody ever asks that question. We are content as we are and wherever we are. It is just one vast endless space, and no time, only bits of eternity."

This was a most unusual statement for the mother I knew below to make.

"Mother, you must have learned a lot since you are here," I said.

"Son," she replied, "there is only one thing worse than ignorance and that is stupidity. I don't wonder you couldn't tolerate me down below. I *was* stupid, terribly stupid."

I started to contradict her but she went on talking. "You see, son, all we have to do here is to learn from our past mistakes, so when we are ready to be incarnated again, we will have learned our lesson. We have all time on our hands here. Some learn faster than others and are gone before one really knows them."

"Tell me," I interrupted, "is there any kind of government here?"

"Oh, no," she quickly answered. "There is no need for government here. We are all capable of governing ourselves. You see, one of the first things that happens to you is the loss of all hatred, all bitterness, all prejudice. Besides, there are no nations here. It is just one big world, one big family."

"How do you manage to live, who supplies the food, who does the hard work?"

"There is no work to do," said Mother. "Whatever you wish you get. Wherever you want to go you have only to desire it and you are there—the place comes to you. Do you remember at home in the storm closet there hung a guitar no one ever played? That was my guitar—but I had forgotten how to play it. Here I have a guitar anytime I wish it and I can play it well. . . . Just a moment and I will show you." To my amazement in a moment there was a guitar in her hand and she was playing it, playing skillfully.

"You sound like Segovia," I exclaimed, full of admiration.

"Segovia is here," my mother replied. "I met him and he gave me a few lessons. One learns everything quickly here. The important thing is Desire."

Suddenly it occurred to me my father was not around. When I asked if she knew where he was she said, "Probably in some corner far away. I haven't run into him yet."

"Don't you miss him?" I asked.

"No, son," she said, "I don't miss anybody or anything. One learns to be content here very quickly. Besides, your father may still be drinking his head off, you know. This isn't Heaven. I doubt there is such a place."

"By the way," she added, "I never asked you if you would like something to eat and drink. If you would it can be served to you *instanter*. You can have Chateaubriand with onions and mashed potatoes, if you like. You always loved onions."

"Mother, thank you, I don't want a thing. I feel as if I had everything. Even the air gives sustenance. It's like breathing an elixir. . . . O, that reminds me, I don't seem to notice the sky."

"There isn't any," she quickly replied. "I have heard people refer to it as an astral sky. Right now we are in our astral bodies. At least that's what I have been told. But it makes no difference to me what sort of body they call it; it suits me perfectly."

"You mean you never have a toothache or an earache, no constipation, no diarrhoea?"

My mother shook her head vigorously.

"Wouldn't you want to stay here forever?" I inquired.

Again she shook her head. "No, son, our place is on earth. We must go back again and again until it becomes a fit place to live. It would be selfish of me to stay here in this Paradise and leave the Earthlings to suffer."

This was indeed a surprising utterance from my mother's lips. I had come in a very short space of time not only to like her but to respect and to admire her.

"Mother," I suddenly said, "there is a question on my mind which has been bothering me. Only you can settle it."

"I am not endowed with all wisdom," she said, "but ask me, perhaps I can be of help."

"It's this, mother. When I was in London some years

ago a friend of mine took me to meet a medium. He was quite an astonishing man, this medium. I had hardly taken a seat, for example, when he said to me: 'Your books have caused a great deal of trouble, haven't they?' No one had told him that I was a writer. He quickly followed this up by telling me that my greatest helpmate in the beyond was my brother. Did I ever have a brother—perhaps one who died before I was born?"

My mother hesitated a moment or two before replying.

"Son," she said, "that man was right. I had a still-born child before you were born. It was a male child."

"Then he's probably here too," I exclaimed.

"Yes and no," said my mother. "He could have returned to earth already."

A man suddenly approached me and grasped my arm. "You are Henry Miller, aren't you?" he said with a warm smile.

I looked at him but failed to recognize him.

"You wouldn't remember me," he said. "It was long long ago when we met. You were still quite a young man. You gave me a job as a messenger. I had been paroled after ten years in prison for shooting my wife. You listened to my story, put me on the messenger force and advanced me ten dollars out of your own pocket. Do you remember me now?"

I shook my head. That had happened so often I couldn't possibly remember them all. Of a sudden it occurred to me that most of the 100,000 men, women and boys I had interviewed while personnel manager of the telegraph company must be here now. I had probably outlived them all. And with that I began thinking of some of the odd characters I had known during that period.

At this point my mother broke in to tell me she had followed my career as a writer to the very end. "I was so happy for you," she exclaimed. "You wanted so much to be a great writer and after much struggle you succeeded."

"Maybe the medium was right," I remarked. "Maybe my brother did help me along without my ever knowing it."

"Many people here were doing their best to help you," said my mother. "You created a stir even in this world!"

"Mother," I said abruptly, "there's one person I would like very very much to meet if she is still here. Do you remember that first girl I was madly in love with?"

My mother shook her head. "I don't think we've ever met. Probably *she* didn't want to meet me."

"Why do you say that?" I asked.

"Because I was never very sympathetic to any of the women you fell in love with. The truth is, I never thought any of them were good enough for you."

"Mother, how good of you to say that! If only you had told me that when we were below."

"As I told you, son, I was a very stupid woman. And then your father gave me such a hard time."

"Do you still love him?"

"Here we don't love in the fashion of earthlings. We make no distinction between one person and another."

"Doesn't that prove rather dull?"

"Not really. Besides, it helps avoid a lot of anguish."

"Strange," I said, "but I feel quite to home here, yet I've only been here a few minutes. Funny, it ain't Heaven and it ain't Hell. And I don't see no angels flying around or playing the harp."

"There isn't any Heaven or Hell, son. That's all poppycock. And there's no such thing as sin either. That's an invention of the Jews which the Christians adopted and have been poisoning the world with ever since. As for Hell, the real Hell is on Earth."

"Mother, you said the *real* Hell. That's something I wanted to ask you about—everything here seems like a dream."

"You're dead right, son. This is the dream world, the true reality. Down below all is illusion. Only the imagination is real."

She paused a minute to point out two men who were passing.

"See those two," she said. "See those cigarettes dangling from their lips. Well, those are dream cigarettes —they taste like tobacco and smell like tobacco but it's only dream tobacco. They can smoke as many as they like, they'll never get cancer."

So there's no sin and no cancer here, I mused. Wonderful place.

"Don't people get punished here for their misbehavior?" I asked.

"No, there is no such thing as punishment here. Unless you call it punishment to have nothing to do but think about the mistakes you made while on earth."

"Yes mother, I call that severe punishment."

"But it's self-inflicted punishment. There's a difference. You see, son, the universe is run by laws; if you break the law you have to pay the penalty. That's only fair, isn't it? Besides, how are you ever going to learn except through experience? You may have noticed, we have no schools here. Here one acquires wisdom, not learning. We live according to our instincts and our intuitions. Like that we remain part animal, part human. On earth the function of the brain is greatly exaggerated. Think of those foolish scientists who talk about light years and billions of stars. That is sheer nonsense. Here everything is simple and easy to understand. Whoever created the Universe didn't intend life to be a series of cross-word puzzles. He made it to be enjoyed. And that's what Jews and Christians find so hard to believe. They wallow in guilt. Even that doesn't make them happy."

"Have you met any Jews since you're here?"

"No, son, I prefer the Negroes, the Pygmies, the Zulus. They are such wonderful, joyous people. And where they lived on earth they had almost nothing."

"You know," she continued, "when I get born again, I hope I am going to be male and black. I get along with those people famously."

I couldn't help but smile. Mother had come a long way from the woman I knew on earth.

"How long do you think you still have to stay here?" I asked.

"It's up to me when to leave. When I've picked the family I want to be born in and the environment. When I'm ready for another go around."

"I hope that won't be soon, mother. I'd feel lost without you."

"No you wouldn't," she said quickly. "That's one of the first things you learn on arriving here. Self-reliance. No more loneliness. Wherever you go you're at home. Whomever you meet is your friend."

I wondered if she ever encountered souls from other planets. And if so, in what language they communicated. I was not too surprised when she said of course they met souls from other planets—even from other universes. They weren't so very different from earthlings—perhaps the eyes were more brilliant and the mind sharper. But though the people from outer space could understand the people here, the latter could not understand the people from outer space.

(I forgot to say the people here understood all earth languages though they might not speak them. It was as if they had received the gift of tongues.)

From what little I could gather about the people of outer space it would seem there was nothing so very mysterious about the universe; the mystery was Man, wherever he might be. *That* made a great impression on me. So then possibly there was something to the Biblical saying, that man was made in the image of the Creator! And consequently an enigma to himself!

After hearing so much from her lips that made sense to me I decided to ask her outright why she had always been so cold to me. I particularly wanted to know why she never had a word of comfort for me when she knew my heart was breaking. Couldn't she help me locate Cora now, I wondered. No, the only way to find someone here was to think hard, wish for them and they would appear. She thought it quite possible that Cora had already returned to earth.

"She was a good girl," she said, "only I didn't see very much in her. I knew you were suffering but I felt that you had to work it out yourself. I always believed in letting people do as they wish, even if they wanted to kill themselves."

I decided to say no more about Cora but to try to find her on my own.

My mother, however, ventured to add a few more words. "The real place to look for her," she said, "is on earth. That's the whole purpose of love—to find your other half. Sometimes the search goes on for a thousand years."

These observations bowled me over. "Why mother," I exclaimed, "you sound as if you had read Marie Corelli."

"Marie Corelli . . . Marie Corelli . . .," she repeated a few times. "Why yes, son, that name strikes a familiar chord. I *did* read her when I was in my teens. I remember one book especially—*A Romance of Two Worlds*. Everybody was reading it then. She was all the rage." She paused a moment. "Why do you ask me about her? Have you read her too?"

"Indeed I have, I rediscovered her towards the end of my life. She meant a great deal to me. Mother, do you think she might be *here*? She only died about fifty years ago."

"I have no idea," mother replied. "But I told you how to find the ones you are looking for."

Her words made me jubilant. How lucky I was, I thought, to be here where so many of my favorite writers were. Maybe they had a club or formed a community of their own. I would look not only for Marie Corelli, but for Dostoievsky, Knut Hamsun, Herman Hesse. In this realm I had more chance of meeting those I wanted to meet than on earth.

But I was not through questioning my mother about the things which had estranged us in life. I realized, of course, from the moment I encountered her that she was an entirely different person here. How good it was to exchange thoughts with her. Below we hardly spoke to one another.

"Mother," I began, "do you remember a woman I wanted to marry who was considerably older than myself? Do you recall the day I told you about her—we were sitting in the kitchen—and you took a big carving knife and threatened to plunge it into me if I said another word about marriage? If, as you said a moment ago, you believed in letting people do as they wish, why did you become so furious, so violent?"

"Because," she replied, "you were out of your mind. It was only an infatuation, not true love."

"However," she added, "you did go and live with her a few years, even if you didn't marry her. And they were years of torment and distress, weren't they?"

I shook my head affirmatively. "But mother, no matter if it were an infatuation, she was a good woman. You should have felt a little compassion for her."

For answer she replied, "Sometimes one runs out of compassion. The world below was so full of misery that if one felt sorry for everyone who was in distress one could shed rivers of tears. When I return to earth this time I am sure I shall have more courage and strength than before."

Having endured much suffering, misery, humiliation, I could appreciate her words. I had one more vital question to put to her.

"Mother," I began, "I have never been able to believe that you preferred to see me become a tailor rather than a writer. Was that true or did you have some other reason?"

"I'm only too glad you asked me that question. Of course I never meant to imply a tailor was more important than a writer. (Though I must confess that since being here I have arrived at the conclusion that one thing is no better than another. I have met some very wonderful souls here, and they were people of no account on earth.) But I am wandering afield. I wanted you to be with your father, to guide him and protect him. I couldn't bear to see him go to the dogs. That's the real reason I wanted you to be a tailor."

"I suspected as much," I answered. "But mother, why did you refuse to read anything I had written?"

"Son, father told me about your books and I just didn't want to read such language coming from you. I knew, when you were just a boy, that you had the makings of a writer. Don't you remember all the books I gave you each Christmas? I used to envy you having all those wonderful books to read. From the time I married your father I never had the time to even glance at a book."

"Poor mother," I said. "And I was foolish enough to think you didn't care about books. How stupid of me!"

She looked at me tenderly and said: "Since I am here I've discovered that books aren't as important as we believe on earth. We have no newspapers, magazines or books. I would say that in talking to one another we are reading and writing books. And we don't get headaches and colitis from it either. Every day we gain a broader outlook on life, become more tolerant and more at peace with ourselves and one another."

"I wish some writers I know could have heard your words. How beautifully put! Now I see where I got my talent from! It was always a mystery to me, always bothered me. I used to console myself by saying that often geniuses are born of very ordinary parents. What egotism!"

Whereupon my mother observed, "Nobody has an easy time of it on earth. Earth is the testing ground. And, as I remarked before, it is close to being Hell. The torment, the poverty, the misery of mankind seems like the vengeance of some cruel god. Here we don't talk of God or gods. Neither did the Buddha, if you remember his words!"

I was becoming more and more impressed with my mother's words. Far from being a dumbbell I found wisdom in her words. Had she perhaps mingled with some of the great writers of the past? There must be many of them here, I thought to myself. But as I soon found out, the best ones had long since returned to earth. Some souls remained only a week or a month, while others stayed for centuries. Thus I soon discovered Dostoievsky, Tolstoi, Walt Whitman, Knut Hamsun and a few other of my great favorites were no longer in limbo. They had learned fast. I could have met Hemingway, Sinclair Lewis, Waldo Frank and the like, even Jack London, but I passed it up.

Knowing my preoccupation with literature, she indicated a certain corner where they usually congregated, but I didn't bother to go. Somehow I was learning more and enjoying myself more, just conversing with my mother. I had abandoned the idea of finding my father. He and Barrymore, his drinking companion below, had probably ferreted out a jolly bar in some out of the way corner.

It is generally assumed that one doesn't know he is dead until some time after his expiration. That certainly was true in my case. Of course, as I have remarked earlier, there is no such thing as time here. Just as one never sees a school house, a radio or television set, a telephone, so one never sees a time piece. Five minutes may seem like a year and a hundred years like a few days. Also, to be sure, there is no sign of automobile or train. The sky is utterly different—more like the Mediterranean and the stars shine brightly day and night. Wild life is also missing, but the air is filled with birds of all kinds, all colors, usually. Singing melodiously. The ground is studded with wild flowers gleaming like rubies, sapphires, emeralds. At the horizon the edges curl up, giving the impression of being inside a limitless pancake. Fatigue is almost unknown, as this astral body is one which never wears out. A very noticeable thing is no one seems to be in a hurry. Nothing has great importance or urgency. Everything seems natural, extremely natural. One is at home and at peace immediately. The scholars and scientists, with their burning questions and dubious theories here partake of a seeming eternal rest.

I had a premonition that my mother was getting ready to return to Earth. I asked her how would we recognize one another when I too returned to earth. She said there was no way. One only *felt* that one had known another in a previous existence. As she spoke I recalled all the things I had heard on earth about reincarnation, karma, and so on. Nearly everyone I knew had experienced some strange "coincidence" at some time or other in his life. Many is the time, in a foreign country, that I had walked the same street before, recognized every house on the block. Also it frequently happened that I ran into someone and knew them instantly. Maybe we had last met in Egypt or China or Africa. Despite all the arguments of cynics and disbelievers, the existence of the soul, the eternality of life, was well-known to earthlings. If there was such a thing as Hell on Earth there was also "Snatches of other realities." Was "reality" not the very word philosophers and metaphysicians quarreled about? Yet it often happened that a simple ignorant peasant or a so-called fool knew more about such matters than the wise ones. However much I wanted to see my mother again, however much I wanted to meet Cora again, I began to feel more and more that I would elect to return to some other planet rather than Earth. Though I had made the best of a difficult life, though I had learned to transform the bad into the good, still I felt that Earth had nothing more to offer me. If possible, I would not only choose another planet but another Universe! I was no longer looking for approbation but for confirmations.

Reflecting on the absence of such figures as Marie Corelli and Rider Haggard, I began to suspect that they too had elected for a different world than the one they came from.

The one thing I prayed I would never witness again was violence. A world without crime, without war or revolution, without sickness and poverty, without bitterness and prejudice seemed to my way of thinking like the only real Heaven. Let the dead kill off the dead, I said to myself. Crazy as it sounds, it made great sense to me. Not a single one of us had had a real chance on Earth. Even the rich were miserable. Even the men of genius suffered tribulations of all kinds. Nor had the good ones been spared. It was as if the planet were diseased, or condemned. *Un monde maudit.* No wonder the brilliant ones were the poets, the madmen like Blake and Rimbaud. No wonder everything was topsy-turvy. No wonder man was beginning to explore outer space—to find new homes for a dwindling humanity, a humanity that had killed the mother which bore it.

The crime of hating my mother while alive now seemed to me enormously significant. I was indeed, as I had written in some book, "a traitor to the human race." The only escape for me was to quit the planet once and for all, find another Heaven and Earth, another God or gods. It seemed utterly inconsequential now to seek out my beloved authors. I knew now they could give me no comfort, no wisdom. The whole business of literature seemed a completely futile one.

If my mother was ready to leave I certainly was not. There was so much I had yet to discover—perhaps I would be detained a thousand years. All the better, thought I to myself. Perhaps by that time no world will be recognizable. Perhaps it will be a new Heaven and a new Earth everywhere, in all the Universes.

During these reflections my mother had slipped from sight unknown to me. I looked about me but could see no trace of her. Had she already returned to Mother Earth? The mere thought of such a possibility filled me with a profound sadness. I sank to the ground and held my head in my hands.

When I looked up I perceived my mother some distance away. She appeared to be on her way out. Looking more carefully, I observed that she was waving to me, waving good-bye.

With that I stood up, my eyes wet with tears, and giving a mighty shout, I cried: "Mother, I love you. *I love you!* Do you hear me?"

I imagined that I saw a faint smile illumine her face and then suddenly she was no more.

I was alone, but more alone than I had ever felt on Earth. And I would be alone, perhaps, for centuries or, who knows, perhaps through all eternity.

Henry Miller
Finis
8/19/76

CHINA

E ven as a boy the name China evoked strange sensations in me. It spelled everything that was vast, marvelous, magical, *and* incomprehensible. To say China was to stand things upside down.

How marvelous that this same China should stir in the old man who is writing these words the same strange, unbelievable thoughts and feelings.

One of the special remembrances I have of China is that it led the world in everything. Whether it be cuisine, pottery, painting, acting, architecture or literaure, China was always foremost.

A rather striking and absurd illustration of this is the fact, so I am told, that in Japan today the best restaurants are Chinese.

There is only one art which to me the Chinese have never developed and that is music. To my Western ear Chinese music sounds horrendous. (Yet when I was living in Paris I had quite a collection of Chinese records left me by a returned traveler. After a time I became somewhat accustomed to this weird music but never infatuated with it.) I may be wrong but I doubt if China ever produced a Beethoven, a Bach, a Mozart, a Debussy or a Schumann.

Recently reading a biography of Genghis Khan I was surprised to discover that his army had penetrated the Chinese Wall (back in the 1200's) just as the Germans circumvented the Maginot Line.

What may sound incredible to the Chinese of today is that, according to some scholars, the great Wall was built in two or three *days*! Every man, woman and child had been put to work, according to the account.

I heard a similarly astonishing story one day in the Egyptian room of the Louvre. The Frenchman who took me there to see the ceiling of the Temple of Denderah pointed to the zodiac over our heads which, he said, indicated that Egyptian history went back 40,000 years, not five thousand, as we are usually told.

We of the Western world are so very, very young, mere babes compared to the Hindus, the Chinese, the Egyptians, to mention only a few peoples. And, with our youth goes our ignorance, stupidity and arrogance. Worse, our intolerance, our failure to even try to understand other peoples' ways. We in America are perhaps the worst sinners.

Think, for instance, that it was not our statesmen who succeeded in opening the door to China, but a handful of young, enthusiastic ping pong players!

When I was first told that I might write a piece for a Chinese magazine—on any subject I chose—I was virtually speechless. Then I became terrified. But finally what brought me back to my senses was the recollection that what I most loved about the Chinese was their humanness. The Roman saying applies to the Chinese even more than to the Romans—"nothing human is beneath me."

This human quality combined with a fine sense of humor are the saving attributes of a great people. I should also add the ability to stick it out, to hold out through thick and thin. In Hermann Hesse's famous book *Siddartha*, he has his hero say—"I can think, I can wait, and I can do without." To me these qualities make a man invincible. Especially "to wait and to do without." America knows neither the one nor the other. Perhaps that is why at the early age of 200 years she shows signs of falling apart.

When I lived in Paris (1930-1940) I was dubbed by my friend Lawrence Durrell "a Chinese rock-bottom man." I have never received a greater compliment.

I always think it possible I have Oriental blood in my veins. And by that I mean either Mongolian or Chinese. Many people, on meeting me for the first time, ask if I do not have Asiatic blood. This always pleases me immensely. I never want to be taken as a descendent of the Germans, which I am.

Even in my writing I notice that I have an affinity with the Chinese. I tell what is, what was, what's happening. I do not go in for lengthy psychological analyses. I think the character's behavior should speak for itself. And yet the writer I most admire is the Russian Dostoievsky. Certainly no one could be further from the Chinese than Dostoievsky.

I wonder how the Chinese take to his work. Is he loved or shunned? To me without Dostoievsky's work there would be a deep, black hole in world literature. The loss of Shakespeare, who must seem like a wild man to the Chinese, would not be as great as losing Dostoievsky.

It is strange that the countries I most wanted to visit I have never seen—India, Tibet, China, Japan, Iceland. But I have lived with them in my mind. Once I tried to persuade a British magazine editor to let me make a trip to Lhassa, Timbuctoo and Mecca without any stops in between. But I had no luck. All three cities seem like mysterious places, and live in my imagination.

I am aware that throughout this piece I have made no distinction between Communist China and the Re-not interested in ideologies or politics. I find that people are people everywhere, even in darkest Africa. When I think of China I think of the Chinese as a whole, not of the things which divide them.

America tries to give to the world an image of a unified nation, "one and indivisible." Nothing could be farther from the truth. We are a people torn with strife, divided in many ways, not only regionally. Our population contains some of the poorest and most neglected people in the world. It probably also contains the most rich people of any country in the world. There is race prejudice to a great degree and inhumanity to man even among the dominant Caucasians. As I hinted earlier, America is rapidly going down the drain. The old countries, poor for the most part, I expect will take over in a very few years. And the people who invented the firecracker will outlive those who invented the deadly atom bomb. We Americans may one day reach all the planets and bring back from each small quantities of soil, but, we will never reach the heart of the universe, which resides in the soul of even the poorest, the lowliest of human creatures.

I am afraid that the old adage, "Brothers under the skin," is no longer true, if ever it were. The Western nations are not to be trusted, no matter how democratic their governments may become. As long as the rich rule there will be chaos, wars, revolutions. The leaders to look to are not in evidence. One has to hunt them out. One should remember, as Swami Vivekananda once put it, that "before Gautama there were twenty-four other Buddhas."

Today we can no longer look for saviours. Every man must look to himself. As some great sage once said: "Don't look for miracles, *you* are the miracle."